HOOVED HOMICIDE

STELLA BIXBY

This novel is a work of fiction. Names, characters, places, and incidents are either a product of the author's imagination or are used fictitiously. Any resemblance to actual persons, living or dead, businesses, events, or locales is entirely coincidental.

Copyright © 2023 by CRYSTAL S. FERRY

All rights reserved.

No part of this book may be reproduced or transmitted in any form or by any means, electronic or mechanical, including photocopying, recording, or by any information storage and retrieval system presently available or yet to be invented without permission in writing from the publisher, except for the use of brief quotations in a book review.

Cover design by Mariah Sinclair

www.mariahsinclair.com

❀ Created with Vellum

For Keri,
Lover of Horses
Best Sister Ever

1

The smile on my face was permanent. Not that I cared. I'd happily take the sore cheeks.

Since Seamus proposed a few days before Christmas, I'd been practically floating in the clouds.

Christmas was a whirlwind of Irish family festivities—a market in our little town of Ballywick, the Christmas Day swim, caroling, visiting Santa, and all the fantastic food and decorations.

The whole holiday was like something out of a Hallmark movie. Growing up, Christmases consisted of my mom and me eating takeout and exchanging small gifts. But with the O'Malleys, the holiday spirit was contagious. From baking cookies with Magella to singing carols while Donal played the accordion, I felt like I was in my own Irish Christmas fairy tale.

And before I knew it, we'd reached New Year's Eve.

At the stroke of midnight, Seamus and I shared a New Year's kiss that put the fireworks show to shame. His soft lips on mine made my heart race with happiness and excitement for our future together. With his muscular arms wrapped around me, the rest of the world faded away. I had wanted to stay locked in that perfect moment forever.

The clock read almost noon on New Year's Day when Gráinne—Seamus' mom—knocked on the door.

"Are yeh awake in there? Are yeh up?"

"Yeh, Mam," Seamus said. His Irish accent was low and gravelly in the mornings. It sent tingles up my spine every time he spoke. I never tired of listening to his dulcet tones. "We'll be right down."

"Magella made brekkie. Then we're off to the racetrack. Wear something warm."

I stretched my arms over my head and arched my back, the soft bedding curling around me. The luxurious sheets smelled of fresh linen and Seamus's woodsy scent. I breathed it in, feeling totally content.

"She's much nicer gettin' me outta bed now than when I was a wee lad." He rolled onto his side and smiled at me. Seeing that handsome face first thing in the morning made my heart skip a beat. His tousled brown hair and stubbly jaw added to his casual charm.

"Can you pinch me?" I asked.

Seamus's brows came together in the middle of his forehead. "Why would I do something like that?"

"Just to make sure I'm not dreaming," I said with a laugh. Sometimes, this all felt too good to be true. I couldn't believe this wonderful man wanted to spend his life with me.

"Nope, still not a dream," Seamus leaned over and kissed me. His lips were warm and inviting. "We best be gettin' up before me mam comes back. The second time is never as nice as the first."

I decided on a pair of jeans and an off-white sweater with the brown riding boots Gráinne had gotten me when I'd first arrived in Ireland. The buttery soft leather hugged my calves perfectly. I was finally starting to feel like I was part of this world.

I combed through my thick blonde curls and added some product to keep them from frizzing.

Examining myself in the antique mirror, I paused for a moment. I was still getting used to my reflection. Not only had I lost a bit of weight since I'd arrived in Ireland, my eyes were brighter, my cheeks rosier. Ireland had been good for my soul.

"I can't wait to meet Rylie," Gráinne said as we indulged in the full Irish breakfast Magella had made for us. The sausage, eggs, and toast aroma mingled into a mouthwatering perfume. My stomach rumbled impatiently.

Gráinne looked like an equine goddess in her perfectly tailored riding pants, stylish boots, and a glorious bright green button-down shirt.

"I'm so excited for you to meet her," I said. "She's been through a lot lately. I think a trip out of the country is just what she needs."

If anything could, Ireland's magic could help lift Rylie's spirits.

"And remember, we won't be bringin' up any relationship stuff," Seamus said.

Gráinne made a motion across her lips as if she were zipping a zipper, then threw the imaginary key into the warm peat fire. Its crackling flames filled the cozy kitchen with a soothing glow.

Gráinne and Donal's eat-in kitchen was one of my favorite places in their entire house. Next to the small round table was a fireplace with a painting of Santa and Rudolph hanging above. The kitchen itself had muted blue-green cupboards with large wooden peg handles. Every time we sat down for a meal, it felt like I was in the middle of a big, warm group hug.

"How's the cottage move coming along?" Donal asked as he entered the kitchen, giving Gráinne a light kiss on the cheek. "Not that I'm trying to kick yeh out or anything."

"We're waiting until after Rylie visits," Seamus said. "We haven't told her that Shayla's not returning to the States."

He squeezed my hand under the table. As much as all of this felt like a fairy tale, there was still the more-than-slightly heartbreaking fact that I'd be leaving my absolute best friend in the entire world.

"I'll tell her while she's here," I said, squeezing his hand back. "I know she'll be happy for me."

"Even so," Seamus said, "we're planning lots of trips back and forth for Shayla and Rylie."

Gráinne nodded. "I can't imagine having an ocean between Sophie and me. We'll do everything we can to help yeh stay close. We can even offer one of the smaller residences on the property if Rylie would like to move here herself."

"Thank you," I said. "I'll offer it. Though I don't think

she'll take us up on it. She has a lot more in the States than I do."

Gráinne simply nodded. We hadn't spoken much about the strained relationship between my mother and me, but Seamus had given her the rundown.

"Look at the time," Donal said. "We best be going to the track. Can't let Collins beat us there. He'll jinx our horses again."

"What are yeh banging on about?" Gráinne said.

"Me nose is itchy," Donal said. "It's on account of that geebag."

"Donal," Gráinne said, a warning in her tone.

"He blinked when he said 'blessings on all I see here' before the last race," Donal argued. "He's up to something, that one."

Gráinne shook her head and followed him out the door, leaving Seamus and me to finish our mid-day Irish brekkie.

2

When Seamus and I arrived at the track, security escorted us to the box seats at the top of the grandstands. People yelled for Seamus's autograph, and cameras flashed as we passed by.

Seamus's family was known for their wealth and their amazing horses. When I'd met Seamus in America, he'd been a park ranger who drove a beat-up pickup and lived in an apartment with several roommates. I had no idea he was part of one of the wealthiest families in Ireland.

All the fame and publicity was something I was still getting used to. I tried not to look at the papers and talk shows, as most of them had done everything they could to discredit me as someone Seamus should be dating. And as we stepped onto the elevator to our seats, a few people in the crowd yelled obscenities about me.

Seamus never let go of my hand. Even without the guards, I would have felt safe.

"There they are," Gráinne said, standing to greet us.

"It's jammers down there," Seamus asked. "I'd almost

forgotten how many people turn up for the New Year's Day races."

"Everything all right with the horses?" I asked.

"Everything's grand," Gráinne replied. "Take a seat here, love, so we can have a proper chinwag."

"Would yeh like something to drink?" Seamus asked his deep Irish brogue in my ear sending shivers up my arm.

"Do they have anything warm? Coffee, maybe?"

"Right away. I'll have one too." He walked away to get us coffee while I pulled my jacket tighter around me. We may have been in box seats, but I was freezing. I still hadn't gotten used to the cold humidity that settled like a fog over the lush green of Ireland.

"See that one down there?" Gráinne said, pointing to a beautiful brown horse heading to the starting line. "That's our Nuggie Buggie Boo-Boo Head."

I laughed. "Your what?"

"All the racehorses have ridiculous names," she said. "We call him Boo-Boo for short."

"Boo-Boo," I said. "That's cute."

"Winds are coming from the east," Donal—Seamus' dad—said in a worried voice behind us.

"Don't tell me yeh still believe those old traditions," Seamus said, handing me a big travel cup of steaming coffee. He hadn't shaved in a few days and had a stubbly beard filling in—a couple of white strands poking through the brown.

"'Tis bad luck," Donal said. "Means the entire year will be banjaxed. Last time we had winds from the east on New Year's Day, Seamus ended up in the hospital an entire month."

"That's because Killian told me to jump off the roof like a goon." Seamus turned to me. "He said I could fly if I believed hard enough."

"He broke so many bones," Gráinne said, shaking her head. "I didn't even know how to pick him up to get him to the hospital."

"Yeh shouldn't have picked me up at all." Seamus laughed.

"I know, I know," she said. "But I couldn't just leave yeh on the ground like that, yeh mad pup."

"All I know is that's the last time the wind came from the east on a New Year's Day. 'Til today." Donal crossed his arms over his chest. "Doesn't bode well for the year."

"Take a gander. Is that No-Name Jack?" Gráinne pointed to the starting line where a horse straggled in.

"Didn't yeh say he had some osteoporosis issues?" Donal asked.

"That's what I've heard," Gráinne said. "I can't believe Sophie would allow it."

Seamus leaned over and whispered, "Sophie is the best equine vet in Ireland. She and Mam go way back."

I'd heard mention of Sophie many times as she was Gráinne's dearest friend.

"I'm sure Sophie gave Tilda her professional opinion," Donal said.

"Yeh think Tilda overruled her?" Gráinne squinted down at the starting line where No-Name Jack lined up at the far end of the row of horses.

"Only cares about winning, that one," Donal said. "Wouldn't put it past her."

"Perhaps Sophie simply fixed the horse?" Seamus said.

"If anyone could, it'd be Sophie," Gráinne said with a smile.

"Tilda's the horse's owner?" I asked Seamus.

"She is," Seamus said. "And fairly new to Ireland, as I take it?"

Gráinne nodded. "She's only been here a few years—came from America—but she's made a mighty impression. She trains excellent horses."

The announcer's voice boomed from the speakers, causing all of us to startle a bit. "It's a grand day for a race."

"There are ten obstacles—fences—over six miles," Gráinne explained. "They'll do two laps and end back where they began."

"Did yeh see Brogan down at the betting booth?" Donal asked from the other side of Seamus. Gráinne craned her neck to listen.

"He has a right problem, that one," Seamus said. "Why doesn't Sophie leave him?"

"She always says she's going to but never does." Gráinne turned away from the conversation and sat still as a statue in complete silence until the bell sounded and the horses raced to the first fence on the course.

"Boo-Boo's looking good," Seamus said to Gráinne.

Gráinne didn't reply.

Donal stood behind her, rubbing her shoulders.

If I scooched forward any more in my chair, I'd fall out of it. I couldn't imagine how Gráinne felt as the owner. I pushed a stray ringlet out of my face.

"They'll come back into view right over there."

Seamus pointed at the opposite end of the course as the horses ducked out of view over a hill.

Gráinne now shut her eyes as if she were saying a silent prayer.

"Excuse me, Mrs. O'Malley?" A voice that sounded like a Texan tea kettle coming to a boil—the shrill hiss of the steam escaping the holes with all the twang of the south.

Gráinne's eyes flew open as she turned in her seat.

"Now he's done it," Donal muttered. "It's the wind."

"What could be so important as to interrupt me race?" Gráinne's face contorted with the unmistakable signs of frustration.

"I've come to buy Nuggie Buggie Boo-Boo Head, ma'am." The man was tall, with a cowboy hat and a five o'clock shadow.

Gráinne stood. "Boo-Boo is not for sale."

"Respectfully—" He took off his cowboy hat and placed it against his chest. "—any horse is for sale for the right price."

Seamus got to his feet quickly, ready to protect his mother. She held out a hand to stop him.

I half-expected Gráinne to get upset, but she just smiled. "I'm afraid money is not as important as yeh might think."

"Is that so?" he asked.

"'Tis," she said. "Now, kindly leave our booth so I can finish watching the race."

"You're an O'Malley, which means you have more money than God," the man said. "But, respectfully, you've gotten that money—and will continue to amass your wealth—on the backs of these horses."

"I'm pleased to know yer aware of who I am. Do yeh care to introduce yerself?" Gráinne asked.

"Vince Johnson." He held out a hand for Gráinne to shake.

"Do yeh race horses?" Seamus asked.

His gaze didn't leave Gráinne when he answered. "I buy and sell horses."

"I appreciate yer initiative. However, yer skills are not needed in this booth." Gráinne turned and sat back down without another word.

Seamus continued to stand, his eyes narrowed at Vince.

"I have a very motivated buyer," Vince continued.

Gráinne closed her eyes.

"And here they come," the announcer said. "It looks like Nuggie Buggie Boo-Boo Head is in the lead with No-Name Jack on his tail. The fences don't seem to slow them down much."

Gráinne's eyes opened, and a smile breached her lips.

Boo-Boo launched himself so gracefully over the fences it looked like he was flying. His muscles shimmered with every movement of his legs.

"They're willing to pay top dollar regardless of the race's outcome," Vince said.

Gráinne still said nothing.

The booth fell into silence, anxiety creeping up my spine. I hated awkward silence. Every part of me wanted to say something, but what?

"At the halfway point, No-Name Jack is catching up,"

the announcer said. "It looks like he might pass Nuggie Buggie Boo-Boo Head on this next fence."

The two horses flew over the fence, perfectly in sync. But when they landed, Boo-Boo sprinted off to the next fence while No-Name Jack seemed to trip over his leg and fall straight on his face. The jockey on No-Name Jack's back tumbled over the horse's head and onto the ground.

The crowd gasped.

We launched to our feet to get a better look.

Vince muttered a curse.

"Get out of here, now," Gráinne said, the look on her face furious now.

Vince returned his hat to his head, turned, and walked out.

The group of us turned back toward the scene on the track.

"We need medical assistance on the field," the announcer said.

Neither the horse nor the jockey moved.

Gráinne clapped her hands over her mouth, her eyes brimming with tears.

Seamus grabbed my hand as we watched the rest of the horses fly by their lifeless competitor.

My heart felt like it might beat a hole through my chest. I wanted to tell them to stop the race. I wanted to run down on the track and check the jockey for vitals. I wanted to wrap my arms around the horse's neck and hug him back to life.

Warm tears trickled down my cheeks as a woman ran onto the course and slid to a stop next to No-Name Jack, falling to her knees.

A small sob came from Gráinne's cupped mouth before she said, "Poor Sophie."

The medics were behind her, some focusing on the jockey and some on No-Name Jack.

I squeezed Seamus' hand when the jockey sat up and looked around with a dazed expression.

"It looks like the jockey will be all right," the announcer said in a grave tone.

Sophie was still at the horse's side. She'd given No-Name several injections in an attempt at revival, but it seemed she was out of ideas. She laid her head on the horse's chest. I wasn't sure whether she was listening for a heartbeat or giving No-Name one last hug.

Several race officials stood at the finish line to divert the horses from the scene.

Boo-Boo came in first, but there was no fanfare. No cheering.

Celebrating when your competition is lifeless on the ground before you is hard.

Gráinne sat, dropping her head into her hands, sobs wracking her body.

"We have to go down to the winner's circle, love," Donal said gently as he rubbed Gráinne's back.

A collective gasp rang out through the stands. My attention shot from Gráinne back to the course.

No-Name Jack was back on his feet with Sophie's arms wrapped around his neck.

3

The mood lightened just as quickly as it had darkened. In fact, it might have been even lighter. It was almost as if a miracle had occurred.

Gráinne hurried to the winner's circle to answer interview questions, listing off her sponsors and thanking her jockey, as we stood to the side with proud smiles.

When the interviews concluded, we headed to the stalls, where almost all the other teams seemed to have packed up and left.

"You guys get Rylie from the airport," Gráinne said. "We'll meet yeh at the house for dinner."

Seamus and I both hugged Gráinne tightly before saying our goodbyes.

As we rounded the corner—leaving the barn and heading toward the parking lot—the sound of shouting stopped us in our tracks.

"You don't know who you're dealing with," a high-pitched voice said. "You signed off on the papers. If anyone looks guilty, you do."

"I signed off on them before—"

"Before nothing. You think you know everything, but you have no proof of your lies. Because they're lies. I knew I should have hired my own vet."

"I understand yer upset," the second voice was quieter. "I'm upset, too."

"Are you? You almost lost a patient."

"*Ex*-patient, who I saved because yeh—"

"Don't you dare try to put this on me," the high-pitched voice screamed. "Don't you dare try to make me out to be the bad guy here. I loved that horse. He was my baby."

"Then where were yeh when he went down? Because I was the only one who ran onto the racetrack to save him."

"Which I could sue you for," the high-pitched voice said.

"Sue me? For saving his life?"

"You said it yourself—he was your ex-patient. You had no right to treat him."

"Would yeh have preferred I let him die?"

"He was going to win. He would have won if-if . . ." her voice trailed off into sobs.

"He shouldn't have even been racing."

"Just get out of here," the high-pitched voice said. "You'll be hearing from my lawyers. And you better hope Milton Millard doesn't drop dead at my next race."

Seamus had apparently had enough. I followed him around the corner to find Sophie and another woman glaring at one another.

"Tilda," Seamus said. "Sophie did nothing wrong. She's the official vet for the races. She has the right to treat any horse in the case of an emergency."

"Who are you? How do you know who I am?" Tilda wore all black, from her boots to her heavy jacket.

"I'm Seamus O'Malley—Gráinne's son." Seamus stood taller. "And Sophie is a good family friend. She saved No-Name."

"An O'Malley?" Tilda shook her head. "You think you're better than me with your prize-winning horses, but Jack was about to beat your ridiculous Boo-Boo. He would have, too, if this hadn't happened."

"I'm very sorry you're going through all this," Seamus said. "It's a horrible day on the track when a horse goes down. But be thankful he got back up."

"He'll never race again," Tilda said. "That's practically the same as dying in the racing world."

Seamus, Sophie, and I gaped at her.

"Yeh have to be jokin'," Seamus finally said.

Tilda glared at us and stormed away.

"Thank yeh, Seamus," Sophie said in a sweet Irish accent. She was probably in her mid-fifties with brown hair French braided down her back and freckles on her nose.

Seamus patted her on the back awkwardly. "Do yeh know what happened?"

"I've got me suspicions," Sophie said. "But it wouldn't be right to go blabbing about them unless they're true. Let's just say I've officially requested that No-Name Jack's blood be tested."

"Makes sense. She'd have to drug him to make him

run with such brittle bones," Seamus said. "She's lucky he didn't break a leg."

"She'd probably disagree with that statement." Sophie sighed. "I suppose she'll take her business to Doctor Collins. He'll do anything for the right price."

"Is that the same Collins your dad was talking about earlier?" I asked.

"Sure is," Seamus said. "He's a right moran."

"He's worse than that," Sophie said. "He'll do anything for a few bob."

"Surprised he hasn't been shut down yet," Seamus said.

"Won't be," Sophie said. "Too connected."

Seamus nodded as if that settled the matter.

"Look at me being so rude. Is this the famous fiancée I've heard so much about?" Sophie asked, flashing me a small smile. "Gráinne cannot say enough good about yeh."

This statement warmed me more than the coffee. My mother hardly ever talked about me. Some boyfriends were shocked when they found out she had a daughter. Gráinne had only known me for a couple of months and was already my biggest fan.

"This is Shayla," Seamus said, squeezing my hand.

"It's a pleasure to meet yeh, Shayla. I can't wait to get to know yeh better."

"Thank you," I said. "It's nice to meet you, too."

"We should go," Seamus said. "We're picking up Rylie—Shayla's best friend—from the airport. She's never been to Ireland."

"Does she know yer leaving the States?" Sophie asked.

"I know how devastated I'd be if Gráinne said she was moving to another country."

The warmth in my body dissipated at the thought.

"I'm sorry," she said. "I shouldn't have said that. I wasn't thinking."

"It's okay," I said. "I think Rylie will be the person I miss most from America. It won't be easy telling her I'm not going back."

"Well, other than to visit," Seamus said. "Yeh can visit any time yeh want. And we'll pay for her to visit, too. Yeh can still be close."

He was so optimistic—and I loved him for it—but staying close would be challenging from such a distance. Dread crept up my spine. I was not looking forward to telling Rylie.

"I'm sure everything will work out," Sophie said.

"For both of us," I said, trying to force the same smile I'd been saddled with mere hours before.

"I certainly hope so," Sophie said.

Seamus and I walked to his hired car in silence.

The driver hopped out when he saw us and opened the door. I slid in first while Seamus told him the rest of the family would take another car home.

"How are you?" I asked when Seamus and I were securely inside, sitting so closely that our legs were touching.

He wrapped an arm around my shoulder. "I'm okay."

"Just okay?"

"Perhaps it's not the right move for us to live in Ireland after all."

"Why would you say that?" I asked.

"I haven't ever had a best friend," Seamus said. "Other than Killian, I suppose, but he's my cousin, yeh know?"

"If this is about Rylie—"

"Yeh can change your mind," he said. "I won't be mad. We can live in the States and visit Ireland just as easily as we can live in Ireland and visit the States."

I shook my head. "Our home is here. Rylie will be okay."

He let out a burst of laughter.

"What?" I asked. "She will."

"Yeh know her better than me," he said. "But when Luke left, yeh would have thought someone purposefully ran over her dog. And he wasn't even her boyfriend."

"But he was Luke," I said. "That's not the point, though. I want to stay in Ireland. I love it here. I love our cottage. I love the horses. I love your family. And I love you. There's no place I'd rather be."

He leaned over and kissed me gently, sending a fresh wave of warmth into my chest.

"But while we're on the topic," I said. "Remember, we're not talking about Luke while Rylie's here."

"Right, sorry," Seamus said. "When are yeh going to tell her about Ireland?"

I sighed. "I'm not sure."

4

Rylie stood in the arrivals area of the airport when we pulled in.

I jumped out of the car before the driver put it in park.

"Ahhh!" Rylie said. "I've missed you!"

"I've missed you too." I promised myself I wouldn't cry, but after all the day's emotions, my eyes weren't cooperating with my brain.

We hugged for what felt like forever before Seamus tapped me on the shoulder. "We should probably take this inside the car so we can head back for dinner."

Rylie had mascara streaking down her face when we pulled apart. I wiped my eyes, clearing my cheeks of my own black streaks.

Seamus hugged Rylie and said, "I hope yeh left your bad luck at home. Me da's already on edge because of the wind."

Rylie laughed and followed us into the car. She tended to bring death—murder—with her wherever she went.

Though, I couldn't say much since someone had been murdered within the first week of my arrival in Ireland.

"So?" Rylie said. "Let me see the ring! Have you picked out a date?"

"June," I said. "At the Ballywick Castle. It's amazing. Everyone in Seamus' family has been married there."

Rylie took my hand in hers and gasped. "That thing is massive. Has your mom seen it?"

I almost laughed. "She hasn't even asked to see it."

Rylie looked up at me and shook her head. "She never ceases to amaze me."

"How do you feel about shepherd's pie for dinner?" Seamus asked, changing the subject.

"Sounds delicious," Rylie said. "I'm starving. That plane ride was long."

"Didn't they feed you?" I asked.

"The food didn't look all that appetizing," Rylie said, pushing her long blonde ponytail over her shoulder. "Though now I'm regretting my decision not to eat the cookies, at least."

"Dinner should be ready when we get there," Seamus said. "But we may have some snacks in the car."

"That's okay," Rylie said. "I can wait. It is so beautiful here."

We all looked out the window.

"And green," Rylie said, then turned to me. "I can see why you love it so much."

My heart lurched. "It is beautiful."

She smiled and turned back to look out the window.

"Wait until yeh see the town," Seamus said. "It's full of interesting people and shops and . . . people."

"It has its fair share of interesting people." I laughed. "And wait until you meet the horses. They're wonderful."

"That's right," Rylie said. "How was the race today?"

I turned to Seamus, who plastered on a smile. "It was touch and go for a bit. We won."

"You don't seem nearly as excited about that as I'd expect," Rylie said.

"A competitor's horse fell. It almost died," I said. "On the track."

"During the race?"

I nodded. "Just as he was about to pass Boo-Boo."

"Who's Boo-Boo?" Rylie asked.

"Nuggie Buggie Boo-Boo Head," Seamus said as if it was the most normal thing in the world. "It's the name of one of our racehorses."

Rylie burst out laughing.

I couldn't help but chuckle along with her.

"They all have weird names," Seamus said, but even he laughed a little.

Rylie caught her breath and said, "I'm sorry. Was the horse okay? Do they know what happened?"

"Probably won't ever race again, but he was okay. They're taking blood to find out what happened," Seamus said. "Who knows if they'll tell us the real reason."

"Unless Tilda was serious about taking Sophie to court," I said. "Then she'd have to disclose the results, right? I mean, they'll show whatever Sophie gave Jack to save him, but they'll also show the other stuff if it's there, too."

Seamus shrugged. "We'll have to wait and see."

"Tilda owned the horse who almost died," I told Rylie. "Sophie is the vet and Seamus' mom's best friend."

Rylie shook her head. "That poor horse."

"It was awful," I said. "Everyone was in tears until he got back up."

"Was the jockey okay?" Rylie asked.

I glanced at Seamus. "I think so."

"You know, now that I think about it, I didn't see him afterward," Seamus said.

"But he did walk off the course into the ambulance," I said. "So that's something."

I held my breath as we pulled through the wrought-iron gate, waiting for Rylie's reaction.

It wasn't every day you drove up to a mansion amid the beautiful Irish hills. I'd been speechless when I'd first seen his parents' house.

"Wow," Rylie said as the house came into view. "That's your house?"

"Me parents'," Seamus said. "But I grew up there."

Rylie let out a little squeal of excitement. "I can't believe I get to stay in a mansion."

Seamus shook his head but smiled. He and Rylie had worked together at the Alder Ridge Reservoir in Colorado as park rangers. It was wonderful to have a best friend and a fiancé who got along so well.

I smiled at Seamus, who squeezed my hand and kissed me on the cheek.

"I think she's excited," Seamus said.

"Excited?" Rylie practically shouted. "I'm beyond excited. This is way better than Shayla described."

My cheeks warmed.

"I'm sure she was just trying to be modest," Seamus said. "It's not like I'd told her about it before I brought her here."

"Yeah, what's up with that?" Rylie said, her protective friend voice clicking into place. "Why did you keep it from us?"

I'd already told her what Seamus had told me, but I figured I'd let him handle this one.

"I didn't want any fuss about it," Seamus said. "I wanted Shayla to like me for who I was, not what I was worth."

Rylie sighed and rolled her eyes dramatically. "How romantic."

"Okay, enough of yeh," Seamus said. "Get out of the car. I thought yeh were starvin'."

He practically pushed her out when the driver opened the door.

5

Rylie was the queen of good impressions. She had everyone rolling with laughter as she talked about her first day as a park ranger when she and another ranger found a dead body in a catfish trap.

Not that a dead body was funny, but the way she talked about her ill-fitting uniform, her first impressions of the fishermen, and the recurring Naked Guy who ran through the park—well—naked, had us all in stitches.

"You're amazing," I said as I showed Rylie to the bedroom one of the staff had prepared for her.

"Right back at ya," Rylie said, nearly falling face-first as she missed the last step. "Oof, I am the only person with enough talent to fall up the stairs."

I laughed. "But seriously, you're awesome. Everyone loves you."

Rylie shrugged in a way she often did when she got a compliment. "They adore you, though. You seem to fit right into the family."

That guilty tug pulled at my navel again. I had to tell her. Right now. Before it was too—

"It's so late," Rylie said. "I'm exhausted."

No, I'd wait until she was rested. It would be better to talk about it when we weren't both so tired. I got way too emotional when I was tired.

I opened the door to her room. She gaped at the space. "This room is bigger than our entire apartment."

I laughed and nodded. Because it was true.

She dropped her backpack on the floor and flopped onto the fluffy, pillow-covered bed. "I don't know whether I'm jet lagged or this is truly the most comfortable bed in the world. Either way, I'll sleep well tonight."

"I'll leave you to it," I said. "Our room is just down the hall, but if you wake up before we do, go to the kitchen and get some breakfast."

Rylie stood and threw her arms around my neck. "I'm so happy to be here. Thank you for inviting me."

I squeezed her tight. "I'm just happy you could come."

I left her to sleep and went to Seamus' and my room.

"How's Rylie?" Seamus asked when I walked in.

"She's probably already asleep," I said. "I'm surprised she made it through dinner."

"What are yer plans for tomorrow?" Seamus asked as he watched me change into my pajamas with a sly smile.

"I thought I'd take her to see the horses," I said. "Maybe even go on a ride? Your mom and I bought her some riding clothes in case she doesn't have any."

"Do yeh want me to come along?" Seamus asked.

I'd never been on a ride without him, though I was confident I could do it.

"I think it would be great if you came." I slipped into bed, snuggling up next to him with my head on his chest. "You know all the good stories about the horses. Rylie loves stories."

"I'm sure yeh could tell them just as well as I do." Seamus squeezed me tight and kissed my forehead.

"I'd butcher them," I said. "Unless you don't want to come."

He laughed into my hair. "O'course, I want to come. Anything to be close to yeh."

I fell asleep with a smile on my face.

Rylie didn't wake up before us. In fact, she didn't wake up until nearly noon. "I'm sorry I slept in so late."

Seamus and I had been playing a competitive game of Battleship at the small table in the kitchen next to the fireplace since the electricity had gone out in the middle of the night.

Donal had come through the kitchen several times, muttering about the winds and Collins and bad luck.

"It's no bother," Seamus said to Rylie. "Do yeh feel rested?"

Rylie yawned. "I don't think I've felt this rested since I was a teenager."

"Yeh woke up just in time for lunch," Gráinne said, coming into the kitchen holding a platter of assorted small sandwiches.

"Did yeh make those?" Seamus asked.

She laughed. "Course I didn't. I got them from the deli in town—they still have electricity."

Seamus exhaled in relief.

"Come on, me cooking's not that bad." Gráinne looked down at the sandwiches. "Though I could never have made these beauties. They're tasty, too. I may have indulged on my way home. They were tauntin' me from the passenger seat."

"You drove to town?" I asked. Usually, they took a hired car, or one of their staff drove them.

"I didn't want to bother anyone," Gráinne said. "It was easier this way."

"Do yeh even have a license?" Seamus teased.

She whacked him on the back of the head, only hard enough to ruffle his hair. "What kinda question is that?"

Seamus looked at Rylie and then at me. "That doesn't sound like an answer to me."

"Just eat the sandwiches," Gráinne said. "I'm heading to the stables. Will yeh be going on a ride today?"

"If Rylie's up for it?" I said, glancing at Rylie. "It's the perfect day since the power's out."

"I'm definitely up for it," Rylie said. "Though I have nothing to wear."

"We have that covered," I said. "Gráinne and I went shopping for you."

"You did?" Rylie took a sandwich off the tray. "How did you know my size?"

"We called your mom," I said.

Rylie took a bite and nodded.

"Then it's settled," Gráinne said. "I'll get the horses

ready. Will it just be the two of yeh, or is Seamus going too?"

"Seamus is coming." I thought I saw Rylie frown slightly from the corner of my eye. "If that's okay with you, Rylie?"

"Oh yeah," she said, her mouth still full of sandwich. "It's fine with me."

"Three horses it is," Gráinne said, not noticing the tension.

Though maybe I was making the tension up in my head. Rylie and Seamus were friends, too. Surely, she didn't mind spending time with him. And—as much as I hated to admit it—I didn't mind having him there, so I didn't have to tell Rylie that the apartment we once shared was now completely hers.

6

We took one of the plushy golf carts and headed to the stables. Not only did it have leather heated seats, it also had a windshield and sunroof. On the side was the O'Malley family crest.

"Ooh, is that another house?" Rylie asked as we passed our cottage.

When I said nothing, Seamus stepped in. "There are several houses on the property."

"And a castle, too?" Rylie asked.

"The castle—yes—it's still here. Though it's being renovated," Seamus said. "After the fire, it needs a lot of work. Shayla is overseeing the project and doing a grand job of it."

Heat flared up my neck and into my cheeks.

"That's awesome," Rylie said. "I can't wait to see it when it's finished."

"It should be finished by the wedding," I said, then instantly regretted it. What if Rylie caught on that I wasn't coming back to the States until after the wedding? That was nearly six months away. She'd definitely know that we were planning on staying.

"What are all those buildings?" Rylie asked, pointing to the small houses near the stables.

I let out a small sigh of relief. "Those are staff housing units. Everyone who works on the property—both for the house and the stables—has the option to live here for free."

"O'course, if they decide not to, we pay them more," Seamus said.

"Sounds like a good deal to me," Rylie said. "Oh my goodness, who is that little fellow?"

A shiny black foal with a white mark shaped like a heart on his forehead had trotted up to the fence. He whinnied and shook his head in excitement.

"That's Cupid," Seamus said. "He's practically Shayla's horse. He adores her."

We stopped the golf cart to pet Cupid. He nuzzled my hand with his nose, and I kissed him on the forehead. "How's my boy?"

As if he understood me, he let out a small neigh.

"Is that so?" I said with a laugh.

Rylie looked like she was in heaven—the same way I probably looked the first time I met the horses.

"Do yeh have much experience riding?" Seamus asked Rylie when we returned to the golf cart, Cupid running down the fence line next to us.

"I rode a few times growing up," she said. "But I'm not a pro by any means."

Gráinne approached on her own golf cart, and we stopped to chat for a minute.

"The horses are all ready," she said. "Sophie will be in with Boo-Boo, so no loud noises. Yeh know how easily he spooks."

Seamus nodded. "We'll stay out of that barn. Is Wes down there?"

"He and Sophie are discussing care plans," Gráinne said before heading toward the house.

"Who's Wes?" Rylie asked, her voice suspicious.

She probably thought we were trying to set her up with someone, but I'd made a promise—no delving into her love life.

"He's in charge of the stables," Seamus said. "He's been here for ages."

Rylie let out a sigh of relief.

We parked the golf cart in the designated golf cart parking area and made our way to the barn where the non-racing horses stayed.

When we walked through the massive barn doors, Matilda, Grayson, and Bentley had already been outfitted for us. Matilda was dark brown like Poppy—her mother and Seamus's childhood horse. Poppy was too old to ride anymore but often went along with us when we rode.

"Looks like Wes got them all ready for us," Seamus said with a smile. "Rylie, you'll ride Matilda. She's a total sweetheart, just like her mam."

"You're so pretty," Rylie said in a cooing voice, sliding a hand down Matilda's nose.

Seamus went to one of the closed stalls where Poppy stood, watching us closely. "How yeh doing, Pops?" She dropped her head, and he kissed her in the middle of her forehead.

"Who are these two?" Rylie asked, motioning to Bentley and Grayson.

"Bentley is Matilda's brother," I said, motioning to the largest of the three horses. He was a couple of shades lighter than Matilda. "Seamus will ride him. And the other is Grayson. He's my buddy."

I slipped Grayson an apple from my pocket. The gray gelding eagerly took the apple and crunched it loudly. "Hey, eat that quieter. I didn't bring enough for everyone."

He didn't do as I asked.

Rylie and I laughed.

"That's not what I said, Wes." Sophie's whispered voice seemed to echo from the roof and down to our ears. "We can't do that."

I looked around but didn't see Wes or Sophie anywhere. The acoustics in the barn were weird—sometimes you could hear a conversation happening at the complete opposite end. Which was what I suspected was happening with Sophie and Wes.

"Why? Why can't we?" Wes asked, his tone pleading. "It would be better."

"No," Sophie said. "It wouldn't."

"Wes?" Seamus yelled out. "Are yeh in here?"

"Shhh," Sophie said. "Don't say anything else. My decision is final."

"Sophie?" Seamus said.

Part of me wished he wouldn't have interrupted. Probably the law enforcement part. I was always eager to hear people's hushed conversations.

"Hey," Wes said, emerging from the other end of the barn with Sophie behind him. "The horses are all ready for yeh."

"Everything okay?" Seamus asked as they approached.

"Oh, sure. Everything's grand," Sophie said, her voice much happier than it had been minutes before. Perhaps too happy. "We were just goin' over a care plan for one of the horses."

Wes nodded in agreement, though he didn't look up from his boots. It hadn't sounded like he agreed with Sophie's chosen care plan.

"I need to get in there with Boo-Boo before the farrier arrives," Sophie said.

"We'll all stay out," Wes said. "Be careful."

"Boo-Boo would never hurt me," Sophie said. "He adores me."

"You may be the only person he adores," Seamus said. "It's a good thing he wins races because he's a massive pain in the butt."

"Yeh just have to know how to talk to him," Sophie said, then turned to Wes. "We'll chat again when I'm done."

He nodded and watched her leave.

The chemistry between them was electric. I'd never seen Wes with anyone, but Sophie was married to Brogan. Maybe all of his gambling problems had pushed her into Wes's arms.

I shook my head—none of my business.

Rylie took to riding a horse like she took to solving crimes—quickly and easily.

We rode through the trees into a large meadow where Seamus had tried to propose but failed when photographers chased us off, trying to get a good shot.

"Is all of Ireland this green?" Rylie asked as we crossed a hill, revealing the ocean in the distance.

"Basically," Seamus said. "And if yeh look at the horizon, yeh can see the ocean."

"I don't have to see it," Rylie said, closing her eyes. "I can smell it."

I closed my eyes and sniffed. I couldn't smell it. "What does it smell like?"

"I don't know," Rylie said. "Salt. Wind."

We both opened our eyes and giggled. It was so nice to be with her again. Maybe if I told her I was staying, she'd stay too. Then we could be closer.

Wishful thinking.

She had her entire family and so many friends in the States. Asking her to stay in Ireland would be unfair.

Not everyone could just pick up and move their lives with minimal interruption.

"How's the wedding planning?" Rylie asked.

Seamus shrugged. "Shayla's been taking care of most of that."

"So far, so good," I said. "I have the cake, the flowers, and the food on order. We booked the venue the day after he proposed. Gráinne is taking care of the decorations."

"Wow, you're really on top of things," Rylie said, impressed.

I continued, "I was hoping we could go wedding dress shopping while you were here."

Rylie squealed, making Matilda do a little jump. She held on and ran a hand down Matilda's neck. "Shhh, I'm sorry. I am just excited to go wedding dress shopping with my best friend."

"Oh good," I said. "I'm glad you're excited. I was slightly afraid to ask since—"

Rylie held up a hand to stop me. "I would have been horribly offended if you hadn't asked. I can't imagine not being there to help you. I think I know the answer to this question, but will your mom be joining us?"

I shook my head. "She's busy with her own wedding preparations."

"Can't say I'm disappointed," Rylie said. "But I'm sorry if you are."

"I'm not," I said. "She wouldn't have enhanced the day at all. I think Gráinne might come, though. Magella too."

"And probably Sophie, if you'll have her," Seamus said.

"Of course," I said. "She's more than welcome."

"Sounds like a fun group," Rylie said, wincing as she shifted in the saddle.

"How's the tush?" I asked. I knew firsthand how hard riding was when you started.

"It's getting sore," Rylie said with a laugh.

"Think we should head back?" Seamus asked.

Rylie and I exchanged a glance, then nodded at the same time.

"Just wait until you get off, and you can hardly walk normally. You'll be all bow-legged." I laughed.

Seamus led us back to the barn, where we hung up the tack and brushed the horses.

"I can't believe we were out there almost two hours," I said.

"My legs and butt can." Rylie groaned as she tried to walk. "You were right. I feel like a real cowboy now."

"That's strange," Seamus said, pointing to Sophie's truck. "Sophie should have been done by now. And where's the farrier's truck? I hope everything's okay with Boo-Boo."

"Should we check on him?" I asked.

Seamus looked torn. "If we go in, we risk spooking Boo-Boo. If Sophie's still in there, that could be dangerous for her."

"What if we're really quiet?" Rylie asked.

"Maybe," Seamus said.

As we approached the racehorse barn, I knew being quiet wouldn't be an issue. "What's going on in there?"

Seamus likely didn't hear my question. He was already running.

Rylie and I raced after him as he slid the large door open.

All the horses were in an uproar—neighing and stomping the ground—but Seamus was focused on one specific stall.

He opened the stall door labeled Nuggie Buggie Boo-Boo Head to reveal a silent Boo-Boo standing in a daze, staring down at Sophie's body.

7

Seamus hauled Boo-Boo out of the stall, but Boo-Boo was so out of it that he stumbled and stepped on Sophie a couple of times before he was finally out. Once it was clear, Rylie and I hurried in to check on her. She was pretty banged up, with horseshoe prints on her face and arms.

Rylie checked for a pulse while I assessed her injuries.

"Sophie?" My voice wobbled when I spoke.

I glanced at Rylie, who shook her head.

I leaned over Sophie's body and tried to feel for breath coming from her nose or mouth, then checked for a pulse myself.

"Is she okay?" Seamus asked from the stall door.

His face fell when he saw my expression.

"Call an ambulance," Rylie yelled over the cacophony. "Maybe . . ."

Seamus led Boo-Boo by the halter out of the barn to make the call. Either way, we needed an ambulance. And maybe the Gardaí too.

"What do you think happened?" Rylie asked.

I glanced back at poor, sweet Sophie. "It looks like she was trampled."

Rylie nodded. "Do you think it could be mur—"

"No," I said, stopping her. "I don't. At least, I hope it's not."

Rylie glanced around and then pulled out her phone. She opened the camera app and showed me. "Just in case?"

I didn't want to believe it was murder. But Sophie had said that Boo-Boo loved her and wouldn't do anything to hurt her.

I nodded.

Rylie quickly snapped photos of Sophie, her open vet bag, and the stall itself before sliding her phone back into her pocket.

Seamus returned with a woman at his side—a woman who made me slightly sick to my stomach to see.

"Hi, Molly," I said to Seamus' ex-fiancée.

"Shayla," Molly said. She was stunning, with jet-black hair, dark eyes, and a neatly pressed garda uniform.

I glanced down at myself. I was covered in straw, dirt, and probably some horse poo.

"This is Rylie," I said.

Rylie held out a hand, and Molly shook it.

"I've heard so much about you," Rylie said, her voice icy.

As the two women stared each other down, my insides got all jittery. Rylie was squeezing so tightly that her knuckles were white. But Molly wasn't letting up.

"Okay, that's enough," I said, grabbing their hands and

wrenching them apart. "We have a dead woman, remember?"

Molly reluctantly looked away first, leaving Rylie with a victorious smile. However, her expression quickly changed as Molly took Sophie's pulse.

"We already did that," Rylie said. "We didn't feel a pulse or see any signs of life."

"Just doing my job," Molly said. "The ambulance workers will do the same. Try not to be offended."

Rylie bristled at this but stopped when she saw the look on my face. This was not the time to have a whose-is-bigger contest. Not that they could have that contest because of a lack of parts, but still.

"Was anyone else in the barn when yeh came in?" Molly asked, standing and ushering us out of the stall.

"I didn't see anyone," Seamus said. "Sophie mentioned the farrier coming to visit Boo-Boo, but from the looks of it, his shoes haven't been changed."

"What about the two of yeh? Did yeh see anyone else?"

"No," Rylie and I said at the same time.

"Maybe one of the staff did?" Molly asked.

"Do you think this was a murder?" Rylie asked.

"My opinion is of no consequence," Molly said.

Rylie had to turn away to hide her irritation.

When the medics came through the open barn door, the horses hushed as they watched what was happening. Molly moved to the side to let them in the stall.

"I'll call Wes and see if he knows anything," Seamus said, then looked at me. "Can yeh call Mam and tell her?"

I nodded and bit my lip to keep the tears in my eyes from falling.

"If yeh want, I can call her," Molly said, her voice slightly nicer than when she talked to Rylie.

Defensiveness rose inside me. "I'll call her."

Rylie stayed in the barn while I went outside to break the news to my future mother-in-law that her prized racehorse had just trampled her best friend.

8

Gráinne listened for approximately fifteen seconds before she told me she was on her way to the barn and hung up.

When I went back inside, Rylie and Molly were in what looked like a whispered argument.

"Everything okay?" I asked.

Rylie turned to me. "She's ruling it an accidental death."

"There's no evidence to prove it was anything but accidental," Molly said. "If yeh find otherwise, let me know."

I gaped at her. "What do you mean if I find otherwise? Have you even spoken with Wes? Seen if anyone else was in the barn?"

"Her injuries are consistent with a horse trampling," Molly said. "Boo-Boo must have gotten spooked, kicked her, and trampled her to death."

It sounded like a horrible way to die.

"What about the crime scene?" I said. "Should we leave it just in case?"

"There is no crime scene," Molly said. "Unless yeh want me to charge the horse with murder. But I'm guessing that wouldn't go over well with Mrs. O'Malley. Now, if you'll excuse me, I have somewhere else to be."

Rylie and I watched as she left, walking straight past a frantic Gráinne.

Seamus tried to hold her back, but she burst into the stall and pushed the medics away with more strength than an average woman of her age.

Sobs burst from her lips as she hugged her friend to her chest. "Sophie. No!"

I couldn't hold back the tears. It wasn't fair. Sophie was wonderful. She didn't deserve to die.

"Sell that horse. Give him away for all I care," Gráinne shouted at everyone and no one. "I never want to see him again."

Seamus didn't respond. Would she change her mind after the shock wore off or not? If Cupid killed Rylie, would I ever be able to forgive him?

I glanced over at Rylie, who was also crying. I wrapped my arms tight around her shoulders. "Never die, okay?"

"Only if you never die either," she said through sobs.

Eventually, Gráinne let the medics do their jobs—placing Sophie's lifeless body on a stretcher and covering her with a white sheet.

The sun was setting, and the barn was growing increasingly darker. The large windows could only let in light when there was light to let in.

"Where's Wes? He was supposed to be calling the power company to figure out what's wrong with the electricity," Gráinne said, wiping her nose with a handkerchief she pulled from the pocket of her jacket.

"I can't get him on the line," Seamus said. "His phone's been turned off, and no one answers at his door. Didn't yeh convince Da to put in generators?"

Gráinne shook her head. "The last time we lost power was years ago. Before yeh . . ."

"Before I left," Seamus said, an edge of regret in his tone. "All right, let's give the power company a call."

He and Gráinne started out of the barn. Rylie and I followed, but the lights came back on just as we walked through the doors. The difference was almost blinding. I had no idea how dark it had gotten without the sunlight coming through the windows.

"We should go back and look at the stall in the light," Rylie said.

"Good idea," I said.

Seamus glanced back and nodded in agreement as he and Gráinne walked out. He was probably taking her back up to the house.

"Rylie," I said. "There's something I need to—"

"Where is she? What happened?" A disheveled-looking Wes came stumbling into the barn from the door opposite where Seamus and Gráinne had just left. "Where's Sophie?" He hurried to us, slurring his words. "Where's Boo-Boo?"

"Have you been drinking?" I asked, nearly having to turn away from the smell of alcohol and sweat that wafted from him.

"It's me day off," he said. "Sophie said—but I didn't want—what happened?"

"Sophie died," I said. "Boo-Boo trampled her."

Wes rubbed both hands over his head. "Stall the ball. I'm not that knackered. Boo-Boo wouldn't have hurt Sophie."

"Wes," I said, "where have you been?"

"At me house," he said. "Had a few drinks and passed out on me couch."

"Did you see anyone else around the barn?" Rylie asked. "The farrier?"

"Do yeh think someone could have done this to her?" Wes looked from Rylie to me, horrified. "Check the cameras. We'll see who did it. They'll rot in prison."

"The cameras likely weren't recording with the power outage," I said, a tingle of suspicion rising in me. I turned to Rylie. "What if someone turned off the power intentionally?"

"Is there a way to do that?" Rylie asked Wes.

Wes shrugged. "Maybe there's a main power supply or something. I'm not sure."

"If someone could have intentionally turned off the power, they might be responsible," I said. "But that's pretty drastic."

"What could have caused Boo-Boo to trample Sophie?" Rylie asked. "Basically anything, right? We were all told not to go into the barn. Maybe that's just what happened. Maybe this isn't a mystery at all."

"Sophie would never put herself in a position to be trampled," Wes said. "Even if Boo-Boo had gotten spooked, she'd have had an exit route. The worst that could have happened was that Boo-Boo could have gotten hurt."

"What were you arguing about before we walked in?" I asked.

"Who?" Wes asked. "Sophie and me?"

I nodded. "We heard what sounded like the two of you arguing."

"We weren't arguing." Wes rubbed his eyes. "Everything was fine."

"But she said something about not doing something, and you said it would be better," Rylie reminded him.

"How much more did yeh hear?" Wes said.

"We didn't hear much at all," I said. "It sounded like the two of you were at odds, that's all."

"And yeh think I did this? That I made Boo-Boo trample her to death, then left her here to die while I went and got drunk and passed out?" Wes looked like he might burst into tears at any moment. "Is that how little yeh think of me, Shayla?"

I shook my head. "Of course not. I just wanted to know if what you were talking about might have possibly distracted her from doing her best today. Maybe she was upset enough about the fight to let her guard down, and Boo-Boo got out of control."

"We were talking about a care plan for one of the horses," Wes said, looking down at his boots. "That's it."

Rylie glanced at me. He'd looked at his boots before, too. He was lying.

"Wes?" I lowered my tone and tried to sound as caring as possible. "Did you and Sophie have an attraction?"

Wes' head shot up—his bloodshot eyes glossy with tears. "No. Sophie would never have wanted to be with me." With this, he turned and stormed out of the barn.

9

Rylie and I waited until Wes was gone to turn back to the stall.

"You don't believe him, do you?" Rylie asked.

"Not for a second," I said. "I don't think he killed her. But there was definitely chemistry there."

"That's what I was thinking, too," Rylie said. "Though if he was the only one here . . ."

"No way," I said. "Wes isn't a murderer."

"People do crazy things when they're in love. And intoxicated." Rylie shrugged. "We should keep him as a possibility. If this ends up being a murder."

She was right. I couldn't let Seamus's connection to Wes blind me.

"What exactly are we looking for in the stall?" Rylie asked.

"If there were footprints from a murderer, they'd have been obliterated by all the people who came through here." I knelt by Sophie's open vet bag. "Can you believe Molly blew us off like that?"

"I'm still trying to wrap my head around the fact that Seamus dated her." Rylie inspected the walls. "He traded up with you."

"You think?" I'd always thought Molly was so much prettier than me.

"Definitely," Rylie said. "And I'm not just saying that because you're my friend. He got lucky with you."

"The only thing in here that might have spooked Boo-Boo is this plastic Mart-Mart bag."

"A plastic what bag?" Rylie laughed.

"It's the name of our grocery store," I said. "Everyone shops there."

"Do plastic bags scare horses?"

"Pretty much anything can scare a horse," I said. "And if Boo-Boo is as high-strung as everyone is making him out to be, then we might never find the culprit."

Rylie looked up. "What about a balloon?"

I shifted my gaze to see where she was looking. A green balloon that might once have been filled with helium now hung from the rafters by its ribbon. "It looks like it's been up there a while. Why would it have scared him now?"

"Maybe with the lights off, it made a strange shadow?" Rylie shrugged.

"Okay, so we have a plastic bag and a balloon," I said. "That's not much to go off."

Rylie moved some straw with her foot and bent down to pick something up.

"What did you find?"

"A nail," Rylie said with a shrug. She handed it to me. "Maybe it came from Boo-Boo's horseshoe? Seamus did say that the shoes hadn't been changed, right?"

I looked at it and then stuck it in my pocket. It might have been evidence, but it wasn't like Molly would do a full investigation now. "If we're going to make a case, we'll need serious evidence that a crime was committed. A nail, a balloon, and a plastic bag aren't nearly enough."

Rylie nodded. "Maybe this will help." She picked up a cell phone from the straw and waved it in the air. "I bet it's Sophie's."

"Is it locked?"

Rylie tapped the screen, but a defeated look came over her face. "Yep."

"Maybe we can figure out the password."

"If we try too many times, it'll disable the phone," Rylie said. "My nephews did that to my brother-in-law a few months ago. It was a mess."

"I bet her husband would know."

"If we ask her husband, he might demand we turn the phone over to him," Rylie said. "Especially if he was responsible for this."

She made a valid point.

"Then we'll talk to other people first," I said. "Starting with Wes."

We tried to find Wes, but he wasn't around the barn, and if he was in his house, he wasn't answering the door.

"We should have talked to him when he was in the barn," Rylie said.

Frustration crept through me. No wonder my mother thought I was a terrible police officer. I'd just let Wes walk out of the barn without getting any information from him.

"Let's go check on Gráinne," I said. "Nothing we do tonight will bring Sophie back."

The realization made me sick to my stomach. Death was so final. Living across an ocean wasn't. Rylie and I would be okay as long as we were both alive.

I drove the golf cart back to the house with Rylie next to me.

"Thanks for coming to visit," I said. "I've really missed you."

Rylie smiled. "I've missed you too."

We rode the rest of the way in silence. The anticipation of telling her I wasn't moving back to the States welled up in me with such ferocity I felt like I might explode. But I couldn't tell her. I don't know why—I just couldn't. At least not right now. There were already too many emotions swirling.

Gráinne was in the sitting room with Donal at her side, his arm around her as she cried on his shoulder. Her eyes were red and puffy. I suspected she hadn't stopped crying since she found out Sophie was dead.

Seamus wrapped me in a big hug when I walked in the door, and Rylie averted her eyes.

"Did yeh find anything?" Seamus whispered in my ear.

"A balloon, a plastic bag, and a nail," I said. "And we talked to Wes. He was completely drunk."

"We saw him too," Seamus said. "He came up here before he left with some of his buddies."

"He said he didn't think Boo-Boo could kill her. At least not unprovoked."

"I would agree with that assessment," Seamus said. "Sophie was a miracle worker with Boo-Boo. He adored her. I can't think of why he'd trample her to death."

"Then we need to poke around," I said. "Talk to some people."

"Tell me more about the bag, the balloon, and the nail." Seamus led Rylie and me to the table by the fireplace in the kitchen to give Gráinne and Donal some privacy. "Do yeh want something to eat or drink?"

I shook my head. "I'm not hungry."

"Me neither," Rylie said, sitting next to me.

"Funny how death does that to yeh," Seamus said, taking the seat on the other side of me. "I was starvin' when we got back to the barn. Now, I can't imagine eating another thing in me life."

"I'm so sorry," Rylie said, dropping her head into her hands. "I didn't mean to bring my bad luck here. I knew I shouldn't have come."

"You didn't bring any bad luck," Seamus said. "Didn't Shayla tell yeh about the murder we had before Christmas?"

"Yeah, if anyone brought bad luck, it was me." I patted Rylie on the back. "Don't be so hard on yourself."

Rylie wiped the tears from her eyes and nodded. "Thanks."

"Let's talk it out," Seamus said.

"There's a green balloon hanging from the rafters," I

said. "It looks like it's been there a while, but maybe without the lights on, it spooked Boo-Boo."

"Balloons are terrifying to horses," Seamus said. "What else?"

"There was a plastic bag in Sophie's vet bag," Rylie said. "Which seems weird to bring when you're working with a nervous horse, don't you think?"

"Plastic bags are up there on the spooky meter," Seamus agreed.

"And then there was a nail." I dug in my pocket and pulled out the silver-colored nail. "Rylie found it in the straw."

"Almost like a needle in a haystack," Seamus said, taking the nail from my outstretched hand. "We could compare it to the nails in Boo-Boo's horseshoes, but nails rarely come out."

Gráinne appeared behind him. "May I see it?"

Seamus turned and handed her the nail.

"This nail isn't from Boo-Boo. The nails in his shoes are copper."

10

After establishing that the horses didn't share stalls, the stall was cleaned every single day—sometimes multiple times a day—and Gráinne was certain there was no reason a silver-colored nail should be anywhere near Boo-Boo, we decided the possibility of someone setting this up to look like an accident was more likely than we initially thought.

"Sophie said the farrier was supposed to be out yesterday. Do you know if he came?" I asked Gráinne.

"Couldn't tell yeh," she said. "Wes usually takes care of all that."

Just another thing we'd have to talk to Wes about.

"Do you know where he'd be?" Rylie asked. "Maybe if he is drinking, he'd be more willing to give us the information."

"He'll be at the pub," Donal said. "'Tis where everyone goes this time of night."

"Do yeh want to come with us?" Seamus asked his parents.

"We'll stay behind," Gráinne said. "But can yeh make sure he gets home safely? We need him."

Her statement sank to the bottom of my stomach. They needed Wes. If Wes went to jail for murder, what would they do?

The pub was so crowded it took us nearly thirty minutes to find Wes.

He sat alone in a corner booth, his head resting on the table as if he'd fallen asleep.

Rylie and I slid into the side opposite him while Seamus sat next to him.

"Wes?" Seamus shook Wes's broad shoulder.

When he didn't move, my insides tensed. He couldn't be dead, too, could he?

"What?" Wes's voice came out loud and slurred. "Leave me alone."

"Let's get you home, buddy," Seamus said, trying to pull Wes out of the booth, but Wes wasn't having it.

"I don't wanna go home."

Seamus stopped trying to get Wes out of the booth and changed tactics to try to get him to sit up.

"Wes, we need to ask you some questions about today," I said.

"I'm not telling yeh about Sophie and me," Wes slurred. "She made me promise."

I shot Rylie a sideways glance.

"You don't have to tell us anything," I said gently. "It was obvious how much you cared about her."

"Not enough," Wes said. "She had to go and die before I could change her mind."

"Change her mind about what?" Seamus asked.

"About us."

We sat in silence, waiting for him to continue, and after another sip of his beer, he did.

"I loved her." He hiccupped. "She loved me." Hiccup. "We loved each other." He swayed, leaning his head on Seamus's shoulder.

"I take it yeh weren't actually arguing about a care plan," Seamus said.

"I always thought yeh were the smartest of the bunch," Wes said, patting Seamus on the chest.

I tried to remember back to their conversation. She'd said something about not being able to do something and her decision being final. "She was breaking up with you."

Wes let out a loud sob, turning heads all around us.

Seamus smiled and waved them off. "I'm sorry, buddy. It sucks to be broken up with."

"It wasn't her fault. It was that poor excuse for a husband she hitched herself to. He found out about us and threatened her."

Rylie gave me a sideways glance.

"Do you think he could have done something to hurt her?" I asked.

"He'd have done anything to get access to her money."

"Didn't he already have access to her money?" Rylie asked. "I mean, he was her husband."

Wes shrugged. "She'd figured out a way to keep it from him."

"So Brogan threatened Sophie when he found out the two of you were involved?" I asked.

Wes swayed like the branches of a willow tree.

"How did he threaten her?" I added when Wes didn't reply.

He shrugged. "Dunno. She seemed scared, though."

"What about the farrier?" Rylie asked. "Did the farrier show up?"

"Dunno," Wes said. "If he did, I didn't see him. I came straight here after she broke me heart. Is the room spinning? I feel like the room's spinning."

Seamus grabbed Wes's shoulders and stopped the swaying.

"Ah, that's better," Wes said just before his face turned red, his cheeks puffed out, and he clapped a hand over his mouth.

I tried to push Rylie out of the booth, but I was too late, and Wes's hand—as big as it was—didn't stop the vomit. In fact, I think it intensified the spray through his fingers.

I was covered.

11

"Did you ever hear from the power company?" I asked Seamus after a long, smelly ride home and an even longer shower.

Wes had refused to come home with us, so Seamus had talked to one of his buddies at the bar to make sure they got him home safely. Or, if they couldn't, to call us and we'd come back.

"They're looking into the power outage," Seamus said. "But it's fierce odd."

"Do you think someone might be behind it?" I asked. "Maybe Brogan or Tilda?"

"Didn't Tilda say she was leaving the country for another race?"

"Maybe she changed her mind." I slipped into bed and snuggled up next to him. Sometimes, it was still strange to me that we slept together in Seamus's childhood bedroom.

He'd taken down the sign on the door that said *Seamus Room. Stay Out or ELSE*, but the framed sports team posters, plaid curtains, and the bookshelf with all his childhood trophies had stayed put.

"Brogan could be a consideration," Seamus said. "Isn't the husband the person the police usually suspect most?"

"Sure is," I said. "And if Sophie cut him off, stifling his gambling addiction, that could have pushed him to do something stupid."

"I still can't believe Sophie and Wes were together," Seamus said. "I wonder if Mam knows."

"I'd be willing to bet she does," I said. "Though it is interesting she didn't bring it up when we were talking about Wes earlier."

"We'll ask her in the morning," Seamus said, kissing me on the forehead and pulling me tighter to his chest. "I love yeh so much, Shay."

"I love you too," I said.

"Are yeh doin' okay?"

"Other than the fact that there's a potential murderer on the loose?" I chuckled.

"I meant with Rylie," Seamus said. "You haven't told her yet."

"I will," I said. "When the time is right."

"No time like the present, love," he said.

He was right.

I needed to talk to her.

Now.

She needed to know I wasn't coming back to the States. At least not to live there.

"I should get it over with," I said.

"She'll understand." He tilted my chin up and kissed

me gently on the lips. "Hurry back. The bed is wicked cold without yeh in it."

I slipped out of bed and tiptoed down the hallway so I didn't wake anyone else up. It was the middle of the night, after all.

My heart raced as I tapped on the door. "Rylie? Are you awake?"

No response.

I knocked harder.

Even so, no response.

"Everything okay?" A male voice asked from behind me.

Startled, I turned to see Donal in his robe on the stairs.

"I just wanted to talk to Rylie," I said. "No big deal."

"She's not in there," Donal said. "She's downstairs with Gráinne."

Panic coursed through me. What if Gráinne told Rylie I wasn't going back to the States?

"Thanks," I said as calmly as I could muster before practically running down the stairs.

Gráinne and Rylie sat at opposite ends of the couch, both with their legs folded, facing one another.

Rylie had her arm resting on the back of the couch with her head sideways on top, and Gráinne was laughing—presumably at something Rylie had said.

"Hey," I said. "Donal said you were down here."

Rylie's head shot up. Her eyes were pink and swollen.

"Are you okay?" I asked. "Have you been crying?"

Rylie sniffed. "A little. But it's mostly because I'm apparently allergic to horses."

"I thought you'd ridden horses before," I said.

"I bet it was the brushing," Gráinne offered.

"What were you crying about?" I asked.

"Gráinne was telling me stories about Sophie." Rylie shrugged. "It made me emotional." She patted the ottoman for me to sit. "Plus, you know I've been an emotional wreck since—"

"I thought we weren't discussing any of that," I said.

"Touché," Rylie said with a laugh.

"Emotions aren't bad," Gráinne said. "Me mam used to say all emotions were perfectly normal. She encouraged laughing, crying, screaming, basically anything as long as it didn't hurt anyone, including ourselves."

"My mom wasn't like that." I sat on the ottoman, so we formed a triangle. "I was always supposed to hold my emotions in."

"I'm sorry, sweetie," Gráinne said. "That must have been hard."

I laughed. "It's probably why I'm so filled with emotion now. I stored it up too long, and now it comes out at random times." I looked between them. It was apparent I'd interrupted whatever they'd been discussing.

Half of me wanted to tell Rylie in front of Gráinne. That way, if Rylie got upset, I'd have Gráinne there to back me up. But that wouldn't be fair to Rylie. She deserved to be able to react however she needed without an audience.

"I'm so sorry about Sophie," I said to Gráinne, trying to break the tension and maybe take them back to the conversation they'd been having.

"Me too," Gráinne said, tears welling in her eyes. "Yeh know, it's difficult making friends as an adult. I've tried. I don't know how I'm going to replace her."

"You won't be able to," Rylie said, her voice hoarse. "Best friends are few and far between."

"How did the two of yeh meet?" Gráinne asked.

"We were both summies," Rylie said. "Summer park rangers at the Alder Ridge Reservoir. And things just kind of clicked. I've never become friends with someone so naturally."

It had been very natural. Rylie accepted me for exactly who I was—who I am. "Rylie took me to her house once so her mom could tailor my uniform."

"Those uniforms were terrible," Rylie said with a laugh. "Mine smelled like dead fish."

I gagged at the thought. "You really need to get them to change their summie uniform policy."

"I'll do my best," Rylie said.

"Yeh remind me so much of Sophie and me," Gráinne said. "It's fun to see the two of yeh together. Rylie, I want yeh to know that yer always welcome to visit."

I cringed. Rylie would know by that statement alone.

"Well, thanks," Rylie said. "I appreciate that."

"And I fully expect the two of yeh to find out who did this to my friend," Gráinne said.

"We will," I said.

Rylie looked at me with enormous eyes but didn't say anything. She didn't have to. She was worried I'd just made a promise I might be unable to keep. I could practically read her mind by the look on her face. That was one of the great things about best friends.

"Speaking of Sophie," I said. "Did you know she and Wes were an item?"

Gráinne smiled sadly and nodded. "How'd yeh find out? Wes didn't tell yeh, did he?"

"He was pretty drunk at the pub tonight," I said.

Seeing Wes so broken had been hard. Under the alcohol-induced bravado, his sadness was palpable.

"I suppose it doesn't matter anymore whether he keeps the secret or not," Gráinne said. "Sophie loved him with her whole heart."

Her words resonated deeply within me. To love and be loved with your whole heart—what a beautiful way to live.

"Then why did she break up with him right before she died?" Rylie asked.

"She broke up with him?" Gráinne shook her head. "No, she wouldn't have. Couldn't have. She was planning on leaving Brogan. Their prenup was ironclad. He'd have gotten nothing."

"According to a very drunk Wes and what we overheard in the barn earlier, she was definitely breaking up with him," I said.

Gráinne stood and started pacing. "We need to talk to Brogan. Sophie would have been worth more to him dead than alive. I told her since the moment they met, he wasn't good for her. Ooh! I have a text message from her saying that if she ever ended up dead, Brogan would be the one who did it." Gráinne raced out of the room, presumably to find her phone.

"I hope you don't mind. I was down here talking to Gráinne," Rylie said, running a hand down her long hair.

"I don't mind."

"I just couldn't sleep, and I figured you were already

passed out after the night you had." She leaned forward and sniffed me. "You smell much better now."

I laughed. "Showers will do that for you."

"Here it is!" Gráinne ran back into the room, holding her phone up like a prized trophy at the end of one of the horse races. "See?"

The text on her screen said almost exactly what she'd told us it would.

"Maybe this will at least get Molly to look into the case as more than a horse trampling," I said.

Gráinne set her phone on the end table before returning to her spot on the sofa. "Seamus talked me out of selling Boo-Boo. He said Boo-Boo was just as shaken up by what happened as everyone else was. Plus, he would never have hurt Sophie."

"Wes couldn't tell us whether the farrier had been by today," I said. "Would you mind calling him—or I can call him—tomorrow to see if he was?"

"It would probably be better to talk to all these people before the news of Sophie's death goes public," Rylie said.

Gráinne and I exchanged a look, then burst out laughing.

"What?"

Gráinne reached for the remote control and turned on the television that normally looked like a piece of framed art. When the screen flickered from artwork to news station, the first thing that popped up was Sophie's face.

"Tragedy in the veterinary community. In a freak accident, Sophie Walsh was trampled to death by Nuggie Buggie Boo-Boo Head," the newscaster pronounced every word of Boo-Boo's name with great articulation, "a champion racehorse owned by Gráinne O'Malley."

A short bald man appeared on the screen with a banner below that read *Brogan Walsh—Husband*. "I can't believe she's gone. The O'Malleys won't get away with this." He let out a large sob and dropped his head into his hands.

"Is that a hickey on his neck?" I asked, pointing at the television.

"Sure looks like it to me," Rylie confirmed.

"Wouldn't have been from Sophie," Gráinne said. "They hadn't been intimate in over ten years."

A thought crossed my mind. Why hadn't I considered it before? "Gráinne, do you know the passcode to Sophie's phone?"

"I do," Gráinne said. "Do yeh need it?"

"Yes!" I said too loudly. My mother would have scolded me, but Gráinne just smiled.

"It's zero, zero, two, two, zero, zero," Gráinne said. "She liked simplicity. And it was so random, no one would have ever guessed it."

"It's in my purse upstairs," I said. "I'll be right back."

12

I took the stairs two at a time, grabbed the phone, and returned to the sitting room before Rylie and Gráinne could start a new conversation.

I typed in the password, but the screen stayed the same, besides the warning message that the code was wrong.

I tried again but got the same message.

"It's not working," I said, handing it to Gráinne.

She tried. "It had to have been changed. It worked just a couple of days ago."

"Who else might know?" I asked. "Brogan?"

Gráinne let out a small, sad laugh. "Brogan is the reason Sophie even had a password on her phone."

I glanced at Rylie. "We need to talk to Brogan ASAP."

Rylie, Gráinne, and I were dragging at breakfast. Magella had prepared a massive Irish breakfast, complete with bacon, beans, black and white puddings, eggs, fried tomatoes, potatoes, and some soda bread.

"This is delicious," Rylie said, finishing the large helping on her plate and going in for seconds. "I could eat this every day."

"Mmm. Same," I said.

"I'd offer to talk to Brogan with yeh, but he hates me," Gráinne said.

"It's probably best we do it alone," I said. "Maybe catch him off guard."

"Just be careful," Gráinne warned. "Brogan's quick as a whip and has a tongue that lashes like one. Sophie was always smarter but could never get in a word edge-wise with that man. He did everything in his power to keep her down."

"Too bad he wasn't smarter about his gambling," Seamus said, walking in bright-eyed. "How late were the three of yeh up last night? Yeh look exhausted."

He kissed me on top of the head.

"It was late," Rylie said.

"Yeh could've slept in this morning." Seamus filled a plate and sat down next to me.

"We need to talk to Brogan as soon as possible," I said. "If Sophie was murdered, he's at the top of my list of suspects."

"Did Wes get home okay last night?" Rylie asked.

"Talked to him this morning," Seamus said. "He's struggling, but alive."

A knock at the door turned all our heads.

Magella appeared from the sitting room. "I'll get it."

Gráinne sipped her tea while we ate.

"Sir, yeh can't just walk in—sir!" Magella's voice grew louder and more panicked.

Seamus stood and positioned himself between us and the door as Vince Johnson—the Texan horse buyer—strode into the kitchen.

"I need to speak to your mother," Vince said, his voice the same hiss and twang as before.

Magella hurried in behind him, the worry lines around her eyes working overtime. "I'm so sorry. I told him he couldn't come in."

"It's not your fault," Gráinne said, standing and moving to Seamus's side. "Apparently, they don't teach manners in Texas."

Vince bristled.

"What kind of gobshite barges into someone's private residence?" Seamus added.

"There's no need for name-calling, young man," Vince said. "I'm here to talk business before someone beats me to it."

"Yeh can schedule an appointment with me, just like all the others in your position," Gráinne said.

"Respectfully, ma'am, how many of those appointments have y'all actually taken?" Vince said.

"None," Gráinne said. "Because Boo-Boo is not for sale."

"I have intel that says you wanted to be rid of the horse that killed your best friend."

"I don't know where yer gettin' yer so-called intel, but yeh might want to be findin' someone more reliable from here on out," Gráinne said. "Boo-Boo is not for sale."

Vince stood there in silence. Gráinne stared back, not adding another word.

I looked between them and Rylie. Rylie didn't seem at all worried about the interaction.

Finally, Vince said, "Name your price, Mrs. O'Malley."

"Who is so interested in Boo-Boo that they're willing to offer any price plus a percentage for yer commission?" Gráinne asked, crossing her arms over her chest.

"Now, you know I can't discuss that with you," Vince said.

"If yeh can't discuss that with me, there's no chance of a deal." Gráinne turned and sat back at the table.

"You've sold many horses in the past," Vince said, trying to talk to her over Seamus's broad shoulders.

"Never with a middleman," Gráinne said. "I like to know who will be on the receiving end of my horses. Yeh can show yerself out."

When Vince didn't move, Seamus growled, "Yeh heard her. Let's go."

Vince still didn't budge.

"Don't make me call the Gardaí," Gráinne said. "It would be a horrible waste of their time to have to remove yeh from the premises."

"Tilda," Vince whispered, then cleared his throat. "Tilda Williams wants to buy Boo-Boo, and she's willing to pay whatever the price."

Gráinne was on her feet faster than I could register what was happening. She pushed past Seamus and had her finger so far in that cowboy's chest that he winced in pain. "If yeh ever speak that name in me house again, I'll have yeh arrested. Now get out."

Vince raised his hands in surrender. Seamus placed a gentle hand on his mother's shoulder, and she removed her finger from Vince's chest.

"Yeh should know better than to think I'd ever sell any of me horses to that cheater. And if yeh know what's best for yeh, yeh wouldn't work for her either."

Vince lowered his hands and gave Gráinne a sly smile. "She pays mighty well. Don't think I'll be leaving her service anytime soon."

And with that, he turned and walked out of the kitchen.

13

Gráinne ranted about Vince and Tilda for almost thirty minutes before Seamus stopped her. Rylie and I hadn't left the house, even though we probably should have, so we could go talk to Brogan. It seemed wrong to leave in the middle of Gráinne's impassioned speech.

Once we were in the car, I glanced at Rylie. "Didn't expect that to get so heated."

Rylie's eyes widened. "She really doesn't like that Tilda woman, does she?"

I typed the address Gráinne had given us for Sophie's house into my GPS and started down the drive. It had taken me a bit to get used to driving on the left side of the road, but now I'd likely have a more challenging time driving on the right. Gráinne had offered the car service, but I figured it would be better if we didn't show up to interview people in what looked like a rich person's car. Not that the car I was driving looked much less rich.

"Did I tell you about what happened with Tilda at the racetrack?" I asked.

"That her horse almost died?"

"Yes, but after that. Sophie saved the horse on the track. Then, when Seamus and I were leaving, we heard Sophie and Tilda arguing. Sophie sounded like she might have been threatening Tilda with something, and Tilda threatened to sue Sophie for saving the horse."

"I remember you talking about that a little bit on the way here from the airport," Rylie said. "Maybe we should talk to Tilda instead of Brogan."

"Or both," I said. "Though Tilda said she was heading out to another race somewhere, which means she probably wasn't in town when Sophie died."

"If she has enough money to pay any price for Boo-Boo, she'd likely have enough money to pay someone to kill someone else, don't you think?"

Rylie made a good point.

"Without being able to check into her bank records or anything like that, though, it'll be almost impossible to find out if she hired someone." I thought about it for a minute. "Unless we can find out who she hired."

"What about Vince? Do you think he could have had something to do with Sophie's death?" Rylie asked.

"He's slimy for sure," I said. "But I don't know what connection he'd have to Sophie. If he simply bought and sold horses, he wouldn't really need a vet, would he?"

"Maybe Sophie would check horses for him before someone bought them. Like a stamp of approval thing." Rylie shrugged. "I don't know. I just know I don't like the guy."

I turned down the road that would lead directly through town.

"Ooh, the town is so pretty in the daylight," Rylie said, watching as we passed the shops. "There are some amazing stores here."

"Aren't they great?" I said. "And there are even more hidden from the naked eye. Like down that alley, an unmarked door leads to a women's poker club."

"Have you been?" Rylie asked.

"A couple of times with Gráinne," I said. "She's a card shark. I always lose."

"She seems to really like you. You scored big time with the in-laws."

"They're pretty amazing."

My throat felt like it was closing up. This was my chance to tell her, but the words would not physically come out of my mouth.

"I feel horrible about Sophie," Rylie said. "I don't know what I'd do if something happened to y—"

"I'mnotcomingbacktothestates." The words tumbled out of my mouth before I could stop them.

"What?" Rylie laughed.

I took a deep breath. I didn't want to repeat it, but I had to now. There was no undo button in real life. I took a deep breath and tightened my grip on the steering wheel. "I'm not coming back to the States."

Rylie turned away from me to stare out the window. Her smile had faded as the weight of my words sunk in. I glimpsed the shock and hurt in her eyes before she hid it from me.

"I know," she finally said, her voice a mere whisper.

"Did Gráinne tell you?" I asked. "Because if she did, I didn't mean for it to come from anyone but me."

Rylie turned back to me with tears in her eyes and a smile on her lips. "You told me. The minute I saw you when I got here, I knew. You look so happy—happier than I've ever seen you look."

I'd seriously underestimated her. "I should have told you before you figured it out."

"Don't beat yourself up," Rylie said. "I'm happy you're happy."

"But what about the apartment?" Mental head slap. "Sorry, that was a stupid question."

"I'll figure out the apartment stuff. The rent is minimal. I'll get a new roommate if I need help paying for the utilities. It'll be fine."

The thought of Rylie getting a new roommate made my insides twist. But what right did I have to be jealous? I was the one doing this to her. To us.

"It'll be okay," Rylie said, grabbing my hand. "Really, it will."

How was she handling this better than I was? Did she not care? Maybe we were better friends in my mind than we were in hers.

We drove the rest of the way in silence, besides the sniffles we emitted every few seconds. When we arrived at the address, I gripped the wheel and gritted my teeth against the emotion like I used to do as a child.

"Don't do that," Rylie said. "You can feel your emotions. You can be sad. Even though you're making this decision, it's okay to be sad."

If it was okay to be sad, why wasn't she sad?

"You okay?" Rylie asked. "We can wait out here if you ne—"

"I'm fine."

Rylie seemed a bit taken aback by my tone, but I got out of the car before she could bring it up.

The striking Irish townhome loomed before me. The gentle morning sunlight kissed its soft, pastel peach hue, exuding a sense of affluence that seemed fitting for Sophie's residence.

Two stories of elegance stretched upwards, their large, symmetrical windows perhaps once a symbol of the couple's dreamy aspirations. Now, they hinted at dark secrets, with curtains drawn in a manner that seemed more about concealment than décor.

I admired the garden—surprisingly vibrant for a winter's day—with its resilient bushes and a few hardy flowers that managed to thrive despite the season. Perhaps they were a silent tribute to Sophie's nurturing spirit.

Rylie's and my footsteps echoed up the path. The click of our heels on the concrete seemed loud and out of place. The weight of the home's somber tales grew heavier with each step. It was as if the house whispered of Brogan's gambling, heated arguments, and secrets. Lots of secrets.

With every step up the concrete stairs, my resolve to uncover the truth about Sophie's death strengthened. I knocked, and the door swung open almost immediately.

"Can I help you?" Shorter than average height, Brogan had a receding hairline that accentuated his oblong face. Dark, under-eye circles framed his bloodshot eyes, and his sallow complexion showed the toll of too many late nights.

Behind him, the dimly lit interior of the home offered a glimpse into the chaos of the time since Sophie died. The pungent scent of neglect, unwashed clothes, and old food assaulted my senses. The living room was a mess—completely opposite of how I'd expected Sophie's home to look. Dirty dishes, half-finished meals, and discarded liquor bottles littered the scene. The haphazardness seemed symbolic of a life unraveling at the seams.

Taking in his disheveled appearance and the state of the house, my suspicions deepened. How long had it been this way? Surely, it hadn't gotten this bad in such a short amount of time.

"Are you Brogan?" I knew it was him. It was the same man from the news report. But he hadn't looked this awful on the news.

"That's me," he said, his words quick and pointy. "Look, if you're here to sell me something, get lost. Money's gone. Well ran dry."

"What do you mean, the money's gone?" I asked, trying to keep my tone light.

"Don't try to sweet talk me," he said. "No matter which way you slice it, there's nothing left."

I glanced at Rylie. Her furrowed brows and frown showed she shared my disgust at the situation.

"We're not here to sell you anything," Rylie said. "We're here to talk to you about the death of your wife."

I glanced over at her, probably with my mouth hanging open. Who was she to take the lead? Maybe I hadn't wanted to show my cards all at once. Then she just throws everything on the table in one fell swoop.

"What do you want to talk about? She was with one of her clients. It trampled her. Case closed. Money gone."

"What do you mean by money gone? Didn't she have a life insurance policy? Or surely you could sell her veterinary practice. Or this amazing house," I said, taking the reins of the investigation back.

"Sophie said life insurance was for people who don't manage their money properly." He tightened the belt of his gray robe around a stained white t-shirt and black sweatpants. "I bet she's rolling with laughter in hell right now."

I wanted to say something about her probably not being in the laughing mood if she was in hell, but my brain didn't come up with a comment before Rylie chimed in again.

"I take it she left you," Rylie said, peeking into the house behind him. "And not recently."

I didn't look at her this time. If I had, she would have seen the frustration written all over my face.

"She left the business to her parents and the rest to a friend. Nothing left for her faithful old husband. What about our debts?"

"*Your* debts, you mean?" I said. "Gambling debts, right?"

Though the sun was out, his icy glare sent shivers coursing through me.

"What do you know about my gambling debts?" Brogan's eyes darted around behind me. "Who sent you here? Who are you?"

Rylie started to say something, but I held up a hand to stop her. "We're nobody you want to mess with."

Brogan leaned in. "Look, I already gave you everything I have. I didn't know Sophie would leave me high and dry." His hands shook. "I'll get him his money as soon as I can."

"Did you tell someone you'd get money if Sophie died?" I asked. Horror probably painted my face like a clown's makeup.

Brogan didn't look at me when he said, "No."

"You did, didn't you?" I asked.

His beady eyes met mine for a split second before skittering away. Guilt was written all over his face.

"I wouldn't have had to," Brogan finally said. "Everyone knew Sophie had all the money in the world. She just wouldn't give it to me."

"Unless she was dead," I said. "Or so you thought."

"I didn't tell anyone to kill her," Brogan said. "I know it looks bad, but she wasn't even murdered. A horse trampled her. It was bound to happen sooner or later."

"How long had Sophie worked with horses?" I asked.

"Since she was a kid," Brogan said. "But they're still ani—"

"And how many times had she gotten hurt at work?"

"Well, never but—"

"So why now? After all these years, why would an animal not only hurt Sophie but kill her?"

"Maybe she was distracted by that tall, muscular guy. You know? The one she was sleeping with?"

Brogan and I stared at each other. It was my turn to try the silent technique. I was mad enough not to worry about the awkwardness. This man obviously didn't care about his wife. How long had they been separated? And why had she broken up with Wes if she'd already left Brogan? I tried to make a note of the questions so I could ask them just as soon as he broke the—

"Do you know anyone else who might want to kill Sophie?" Rylie asked. "Besides the guys you owe money?"

Frustration turned to anger. She was ruining everything. The silent technique would have worked.

I almost said something right then and there, but I didn't want to seem unprofessional. Not that I was a professional *anything*.

In fact, I was no better than the man in front of me. I had no job either—I was living off Seamus. He had insisted multiple times that I didn't need to worry about it, that he had it covered. But what if he died? We weren't even married. I'd have to go back to the States with a broken heart and start all over.

Rylie nudged me.

"Sorry. I missed that," I said.

"He said he thinks Tilda could have killed Sophie," Rylie said.

"Tilda was out of the country," I said. "Is there anyone else?"

"Tilda might have been out of the country, but what about her jockey? Or maybe she hired someone to do it. She had more money than any one person needed."

"Let's assume Tilda is responsible," I said. "What's her motive?"

"Did you see the New Year's Day race? Her prized racehorse almost dropped dead."

"I saw it," I said. "And I saw them arguing afterward."

"Sophie told me about it when she got home." Brogan nodded with his eyes wide. I couldn't tell whether he was lying. "And that's why I think Tilda killed her. I mean, if she was murdered, that is."

Rylie opened her mouth, but before she could say anything, I said, "Thank you for your time."

"Uh, yes, thank you," Rylie said before following me down the steps.

Once we were encased in the car, Rylie turned to me with a look of pure confusion on her face. "What in the world is going on with you?"

14

"What's up with me? What's up with you?" I said, deflecting Rylie's question back to her.

"I was just trying to help," Rylie said. "But you don't seem to want my help."

"This is *my* investigation. Mine. This is my future mother-in-law's best friend. I know the two of you had a great time last night without me, but that doesn't mean you can just waltz in here and take over everything."

I thought I'd feel better getting my feelings out in the open, but the minute the words were out, I wanted them magically to go back inside my mouth and be forgotten forever.

Rylie sat staring at the dashboard for such a long time, I wondered if maybe I hadn't actually said those words. Maybe this was all just a dream. I pinched my leg hard enough to know it wasn't.

"I'm sorry you feel like I came in here to take over,"

Rylie finally said, her voice shaking slightly. "I guess I'm just used to taking the lead. I'll do better in the future."

I'd won, but I felt like a loser. "I'm sorry. I shouldn't have yelled at you."

"It's okay," Rylie said. "You're right. I need to know my place."

I groaned. "That's not what I was trying to say. Can we just forget this happened? Get a drink at the pub?"

Rylie put a fake smile on her face. "Yeah, that sounds fun."

Thankfully, as usual, the pub was busy and noisy enough to make our lack of conversation less noticeable. We squeezed our way to an open high-top table near the bar.

Harry, the pub's owner, brought us each a pint of Guinness without me even having to ask. Rylie wasn't usually a Guinness drinker, but some things were necessities when in Ireland. One of those was experiencing a Guinness in a local pub, and we hadn't managed to do that with Wes last night.

"It's better than I expected," Rylie said after the first sip. "Though I thought it would taste like root beer with how it looks."

I sipped my beer and smiled. "I'm glad you like it. So, what do you think about Brogan?"

"He may not have killed her, but he easily could have dropped hints that he'd have money if she were dead," Rylie said.

"What I can't quite figure out is why she would have

broken up with Wes and where she was staying. There's no way she was living in that filth or that it's gotten that dirty and smelly since she's been dead."

"If she were staying with Wes, her stuff would still be there," Rylie said.

"Shoot, I forgot to bring up the cell phone," I said. "I thought Brogan might know what the new passcode could be."

"Even if he had known, he wouldn't have told us."

The bar erupted in cheers. The ancient boxy TV suspended above the bar showed a grainy picture of a horse racing to the finish line.

"Does Gráinne not race in all the races?" Rylie asked.

"I'm not sure," I said. "Maybe they went without her this time. I imagine she'd want to stay home after what happened with Sophie."

"Shh," a man from behind us yelled. "I wanna hear what the American broad says about her second win in a row."

The bar went quiet, and Harry turned the sound up on the TV.

"How does it feel to win two races in a row after the horrible New Year's Day catastrophe?" The sports reporter held a mic up to Tilda's mouth.

"New Year's Day was a terrible day." She frowned. "I didn't think we'd bounce back from it. No-Name Jack was the only horse I'd deemed fit to race. Thankfully, my new jockey brought my attention to one of the horses I never thought would race." She reached up and patted the horse's face, who stood to her left. "But Milton Millard proved me wrong."

A man at the bar shook his head. "Turn it off. We don't need to hear anymore."

Harry quickly muted the TV. A couple of people booed, but eventually, the bar returned to its noisy hum.

"Is that No-Name Jack's jockey?" Rylie said, almost hesitant.

"Where?" I asked, feeling slightly stupid I hadn't recognized him. I mean, I was the one at the race, not Rylie.

"At the bar," Rylie said. "I think he's the one who told the owner to turn it off."

I squinted. He still didn't look familiar. "How do you know what he looks like?"

"Gráinne showed me the race replay last night," Rylie said sheepishly. "You know, just to get me caught up."

I hated that I'd made my best friend walk on eggshells around me.

"They zoomed in on the jockey's face when Sophie was reviving No-Name Jack. He seemed devastated."

"Maybe we can get some information out of him," I said, wiggling my eyebrows at Rylie.

"Ooh, good idea," she said, though I was reasonably sure she'd already had that idea several steps before me.

Even though I had been the police officer, Rylie had been on more actual murder cases. It only made sense she'd have a knack for solving crimes. Not that I felt any better because of that, but still.

"How should we play it?" I asked, extending an olive branch.

"Are you sure? I don't want to step on your toes,"

Rylie's voice was completely sarcasm-free. She seemed genuinely bummed about upsetting me.

"I'm positive," I said. "What's the plan?"

"Since I'm new to town, I could play the dumb tourist and flirt with him. Maybe he'll get drunk and tell me everything."

"It's worth a shot."

Rylie downed the rest of her beer, threw her shoulders back, and plastered an unnaturally large smile on her face. "How's this?" she asked in a high-pitched voice as she batted her eyelashes.

"It's scary how good you are at that."

"Wish me luck." She walked to the bar with an airiness I didn't know was possible from her.

I tried to listen to their conversation, but the bar was too loud, so I just watched and sipped my beer.

Rylie went in hard with big, flashy smiles, fluttering eyelashes, and the tried-and-true bicep squeeze.

I couldn't tell how the jockey was taking Rylie's antics with his back to me. He must have been talking to her, though, because she seemed to stop and listen occasionally.

When he finally turned to look at her, he was smiling.

Score one for Rylie.

15

Either Rylie was a better actress than I gave her credit for, or she was actually into the jockey.

"Yeh poking around in Sophie's death?" Harry asked, his voice barely audible over the noisy bar atmosphere.

"Maybe." I took a sip of the Guinness he had just delivered.

"If I were you, I'd look at Wes," Harry said. "Don't be gettin' me wrong, I like Wes, but everyone knew they were seeing each other behind her husband's back."

"Her husband with gambling debts high enough to make someone want to kill his wife?" I asked.

Harry let out a low whistle. "Never thought of that angle."

I shrugged. "Why would Wes kill her if they were seeing each other?" He didn't have to know that Wes and Sophie had recently broken up.

"Dunno," Harry said. "But he came stumbling in here drunk last night, proclaiming to the world that it was his fault she was dead. Yeh know, before the three of yeh came and dragged him outta here."

My stomach dropped, leaving me slightly nauseous. "He said that?"

Harry didn't reply.

He simply shrugged and walked away.

I wanted it not to be Wes. Primarily for Seamus' sake but also for mine. Wes was one of the nicest people I'd met in Ireland. I couldn't imagine him killing anyone.

"You won't believe this," Rylie said, startling me out of my thoughts.

"What?"

"He said Tilda and Vince worked with the local vet on all their horse deals," Rylie said.

"Do you think he meant Sophie?" I asked. "There's another vet—Doctor Collins, I think. Donal mentioned him jinxing their horses. Maybe he meant that one."

"Do you want me to go ask?" Rylie turned back to the bar, but the jockey was gone. "Where'd he go? Did you see him leave?"

I shook my head. "I was too busy listening to Harry tell me that Wes practically announced to the entire bar that he was responsible for her death."

"What?" Rylie's eyes widened. "Do you think it was a confession?"

I shook my head. "Not really. He was probably thinking that he should have stayed near the barn to protect her or something. But who knows? We'll need to talk to him again when he's sober. If he did do it, it'll kill Seamus. They're really close. It would almost be like if he told me you killed someone."

"Yeah, that would be silly," Rylie said. "If I killed anyone, you'd be the first to know."

I rolled my eyes for dramatic effect but couldn't keep from smiling at her joke. "Did you learn anything about Tilda besides her connection with Vince and a vet?"

"Nope," Rylie said. "He has a non-disclosure agreement. He can't mutter a word about their partnership, or Tilda could take him for everything he's worth. Even him telling me about Vince and the vet was probably pushing it."

"You couldn't persuade him with your flirtations?"

She shook her head. "I did my best, but he's gay."

"That would definitely make it harder to persuade him."

"I know it's tough, but we should look into Wes. At least to rule him out." Rylie's voice was tentative.

"First, I want to talk to Brogan again," I said. "My emotions got in the way before, and I shouldn't have let him off so easily. If anything, maybe he can give us an idea of who has been after him for money."

"Maybe," Rylie said.

I waved at Harry as we walked out of the bar.

"I probably shouldn't drive," I said. "I had two drinks."

"Same," Rylie said. "Could you call that fancy car company?"

I shifted my weight from one foot to the other. "Do you think I'm the same as Sophie's husband?"

"In what way?" Confusion spread over Rylie's face.

"I don't have a job. I'm basically just freeloading off Seamus."

"Do you think Seamus wants you to get a job?"

"Maybe," I said. "I don't know."

"You should ask him," Rylie said. "Be honest about your feelings and open when he tells you his. If I had to guess, he's not expecting you to get a job right now, but maybe in the future. Unless you're planning on starting a family right away and want to stay home with your kids."

A smile came over my face. "We definitely want kids. I don't know how soon, though."

"Just talk to him," Rylie said. "And if you don't think he's being straight with you, talk to Gráinne or Donal. They seem kind but also straightforward. They'll tell you what they think."

She was right. I needed to communicate. Which I would do . . . eventually. But right now, I needed a car.

I pulled out my phone and dialed the car service. "They said they'd be here in five minutes."

Rylie nodded. "You know, even though that jockey couldn't tell me anything when I asked about Tilda, he winced as if just thinking about her pained him."

"If only Tilda were in town that day, it would be a no-brainer."

"Maybe she was," Rylie said. "If she's as rich as she comes off, she could have easily chartered a flight here and back. It would have made for the perfect alibi."

"But wouldn't there be flight records? Even private jets have to keep logs, don't they?"

Rylie shrugged. "I think so. It's just a matter of getting our hands on them."

The car pulled up and had us to Brogan's house in no time.

Maybe it was the liquid courage from the Guinness, or

maybe I was more inclined to get the truth out of this guy so we didn't have to implicate Wes. Either way, I was ready for some action.

I knocked on the door with authority. Within seconds, I heard footsteps approaching.

I had to double-check we were at the right house when a woman in what looked like nothing but a silk robe opened the door.

"Uh, is Brogan here?" I asked, confusion chipping away at my courage.

"Yeah, let me get him." She turned and walked back into the disgusting house. Definitely the same one from earlier. "Brogan, there are some lasses at the door for yeh. Yeh better not have called multiple women again."

"Yer the only one I called," Brogan said, appearing from what looked like a stairway. His face went white when he saw us. "What are yeh doing here? I already told yeh everything—"

"So much for being a loyal husband," I said, not even trying to hold back the disgust in my voice. "You seem to have moved on pretty quickly."

"Moved on? Honey, I'm the original," the woman said. Her grating voice only added to the cacophony of dysfunction. I scrutinized her closer. Strands of platinum blonde hair hung limply from her greasy roots, and the revealing outfit she sported looked like something dug out of a donations pile, not the wardrobe of a kept woman. This was all wrong.

"Will you shut up?" Brogan said to her, then turned back to Rylie and me. "C'mere 'til I tell yeh, we both had our indiscretions."

I glared at him. He and I were definitely different. I'd never cheat on Seamus.

Rylie shifted beside me.

"Is that why you killed her?" I asked. "Because you were angry she'd had an affair."

"Killed her?" The woman gasped. "He didn't kill anyone. He was with me when Sophie died and the night before that."

"Do you have any proof of that?"

"We were at the casino with Arnold. Brogan was winning."

I tilted my head and narrowed my eyes at Brogan. "Did you use the money to pay off the debts you owed?"

"Debts?" The woman laughed. "Brogan always won. And if not, he had plenty of money to lose."

"She doesn't know, does she?" I asked.

"What don't I know?" She stared at Brogan.

"He's broke," I said. "Every penny of Sophie's money is going somewhere else."

"Broke? Sophie's money?" The woman's face contorted in confusion. "He had his own money. He didn't need none of Sophie's. They were nothing. He didn't even care when she cut him off."

Ah, so she did cut him off. "How long ago did that happen?"

"Last we—"

Brogan interrupted her. "Will yeh shut yer gob?"

"Interesting timing," I said. "She cut you off, and then she ends up dead?"

The woman clapped a hand over her mouth.

"She already told yeh, we have alibis for that night."

"Right, you were with Arnold at the casino," I said. "Is he your bookie? The one who might have killed your wife, so you'd inherit her money and be able to pay him back?"

Brogan's left eye twitched at the mention of Arnold's name. Had I struck a nerve?

The woman began pulling on her clothes. "This is a right handful. I don't be needin' this kind of carry-on in me life."

"Come on, don't go acting the maggot," Brogan said. "I love yeh. We can be together now."

"Yeh can go and bollox if yeh think I'm doin' that," she said. "I'm not an eejit like Sophie was. Yer not gonna mooch off me."

Her brashness surprised me. For all her faults, she seemed to have some self-respect. Brogan, on the other hand, looked utterly pathetic, pleading with her not to leave.

He reached for her as she walked past him and then us.

"Delete me number," she said over her shoulder.

Brogan watched as she got into a car parked down the street and sped off.

"Yeh won't go tryin' to talk to Arnold if yeh know what's good for yeh."

With that, he slammed the door in our faces.

16

We asked the driver to take us to the nearest casino.

The engine's purr seemed almost too smooth, too polished for the surroundings as we ventured farther from Ballywick's affluence. Our car, a beacon of luxury, cut a stark contrast against the backdrop of Loughbryn—the neighboring town—whose streets told tales of simpler times and harder lives. The transition was palpable: from pristine lanes to cobbled pathways scarred by years of use.

Gazing out the window, I watched locals in their tattered winter garb stop in their tracks to steal curious, sometimes wary, glances at our vehicle. Their eyes, though lined with resilience, held an underlying caution.

Above, the once-warm winter sun hid behind a curtain of imposing clouds, casting a foreboding gloom over the town. An impending rain seemed to threaten more than just wet streets—it echoed the storm anxiety brewing within me.

As the car wove through the maze-like streets, my heart raced. I was on my way to face a bookie at the casino the driver called the Gaelic Gold Grotto. This man could be entwined in dark dealings and debts, possibly even murder. Every turn we took felt like a descent further into a world I wasn't sure I was ready for. The town, with its raw and unvarnished authenticity, suddenly felt menacing, mirroring the trepidation building in my chest. Would I find answers in Loughbryn, or was I simply opening the door to even greater danger?

"You okay?" Rylie asked, snapping me out of my thoughts.

"I have a bad feeling about this," I said.

"What kind of bad feeling?"

"There's something about this town that's just . . . I don't know."

"It's not as posh as Ballywick," Rylie agreed. "We don't have to talk to this guy. We could let Molly handle it."

Would Molly do anything about it, though? I hadn't given her any of the information I'd gotten, mostly because I didn't think it would change her mind. But there might have been a small part of me that wanted the glory of saying I solved a murder that she didn't even think was a murder in the first place.

"We'll be okay," I said.

Rylie nodded in agreement.

As we turned a sharp corner, missing the crumbling curb by mere inches, the Gaelic Gold Grotto came into view. This wasn't the sprawling, opulent casino of Las Vegas, shimmering with lights and grandeur. Instead, it was a modest establishment tucked between two other shops.

Doyle's Pawn and Trade stood on the right. The dimly lit shop had a hodgepodge of items displayed haphazardly in its window — from old musical instruments to tarnished jewelry.

On the left, a faded wooden sign read Blackthorn's Herbal Remedies above a rundown shop, its windows lined with rows of dark-colored bottles and bundles of dried herbs. A man cautiously entered, exchanging a furtive glance with a woman who was exiting before disappearing inside.

There were no grand fountains or luxurious archways in front of the Gaelic Gold Grotto, just a straightforward entrance with a few locals milling about outside. Peeking through the windows, a few lonely slot machines stood as silent sentinels to secrets hidden within.

When the driver stopped to let us out, the people under the chipping gold sign craned their necks to see who was exiting.

"Do you want me to come inside with you?" The driver asked when he opened the door for Rylie and me. The thing about Gráinne's drivers was they doubled as security.

"We'll be okay," I said. "Thank you."

"I'll be right here. You have my number if you need me." He closed the door behind us and leaned against the car, his eyes taking in the surroundings.

Rylie let me take the lead, but part of me wished she hadn't. She was so much braver than I was. But I'd made it clear that this was my investigation, and I needed to follow through with that.

The casino was busier than I expected for mid-afternoon on a work day. A rush of warm, stale air greeted me as I pushed open the door. The faint hum of conversations and the occasional cheer from a winning bet blended into the background.

Dim overhead lights cast a golden hue, making the room feel both intimate and slightly foreboding. The plush carpet—the red turned pink from years of foot traffic—led me past rows of clinking slot machines, their bright screens flashing enticingly.

Dark wooden tables, surrounded by eager gamblers, held card games and roulette wheels. A large bar to my left was lined with patrons sipping dark ales and whiskey, while a small stage at the back showcased a local musician strumming a melancholy tune.

Everywhere I looked, patrons seemed engrossed in their games, their faces a mask of hope, desperation, or resignation. The weight of secrets and untold stories seemed to hang in the air.

"How are we going to find Arnold?" Rylie asked, looking around.

"Arnold?" a tiny old man at a slot machine near us asked without taking his eyes off the screen.

Rylie glanced at me, and I shrugged.

"He's a bookie," I said, approaching the man.

"Why do yeh want to get involved with such a gobshite like Arnold?"

"We have a friend who recommended him," I said. "Is he here?"

The man pulled his hand off the machine as if it was physically painful to do so and turned toward us in his swivel seat. "Yer lookin' at 'im."

"You're Arnold, the bookie?" Rylie asked, not even trying to mask her surprise.

"What'd yeh expect?" Arnold asked.

Rylie shrugged and thankfully didn't answer.

"Who told yeh about me?" Arnold asked.

"Brogan Walsh," I said. "Told us you were the best in the business."

"Yeh don't need to be lyin' to me, missy. Brogan wouldn't have said that."

"He said he owed you money," I said, trying a different angle.

"He does," Arnold said. "Heaps of it. Said he'd get it from the moneybags wife, but she's dead now."

"That's why we're here," I said. "There's a possibility she was murdered."

"And yeh think Brogan did it?" Arnold asked.

"Or someone who thought Brogan might get a tidy settlement if she died," I said.

Arnold narrowed his eyes at me. "Are yeh suggesting I had something to do with Brogan's wife's death?"

"You would benefit if she died—or at least you might have thought you would," I said.

He stared for a few more seconds before he started laughing.

I wanted to but didn't look at Rylie. She was probably just as confused as I was.

"What's funny about that?" I asked.

Arnold pushed himself off the stool to reveal that the

hunch he had while sitting didn't amend when he stood. "Someone of my physical nature couldn't possibly kill a woman."

"Maybe you have people working for you to collect on your debts," Rylie said.

He sat back down and shook his head. "Americans. So dramatic. I don't have people working for me. This isn't New York City, if yeh couldn't tell."

"What kind of bookie doesn't have people who collect on gamblers' debts?" I asked.

"The kind who doesn't need them," Arnold said. "I've enough money to keep me going. And I believe what goes around comes around."

This guy was full of crap. I glanced at Rylie, who crossed her arms over her chest.

"How do we know you're actually Arnold?" I asked. "Maybe we should ask around."

"These people don't know me," he said.

"I'll go ask at the bar," Rylie said.

"Okay, fine, I'm not the Arnold you're looking for," he said. "But my name is Arnold."

"Can you tell us where to find the one we're looking for?" I asked, trying to push away my frustrations.

"Nope." He turned back to the slot machine and started pressing buttons again.

Of course, it couldn't have been that easy, could it?

"Are these ladies bothering you, Arnie?" A young woman with bright orange hair and a nametag that read Bunny walked up, holding a tray of empty glasses. She wore a black, fitted dress that accentuated her slender figure, paired with comfortable, worn-in shoes that hinted at the long hours she spent on her feet. A vintage silver locket rested just above her collarbone.

"Not anymore, they aren't," he said. "I'll take another."

She took the empty glass he handed her, then turned her attention to us. "What do yeh want?"

"We're looking for the bookie named Arnold," I said.

Bunny gave me a sly grin and motioned with her head to walk with her. Her movements were graceful and practiced as she navigated between the rows of slot machines.

When we were out of earshot of Arnie, she said, "He loves messing with people. Imagine him as a bookie. He wouldn't make it a week."

Something about her made me feel like she wasn't telling the whole truth, either. Maybe it was just the atmosphere of the dark building as we inched farther into its depths.

"What do you want with Arnold anyway?" she asked.

"He did some business with a person of interest in a murder investigation," I said, not bothering to hide the truth. I wanted to see expression when I mentioned murder.

Most people would recoil from the thought, but not Bunny. She acted like murder was something people talked about every day on the regular. She simply laughed and said, "Which one?"

Now, it was my turn to keep my surprise in check. "Sophie Walsh. A vet from Ballywick."

"Yeh think Arnold and his goons had something to do with her death?" Bunny asked, grabbing a glass from an empty table and depositing it among the growing circle on her tray. "Thought she got stepped on by a horse."

I shrugged. "Maybe she did. Or maybe there's more to the story."

"Look, you're gonna need more than that to get close to Arnold," Bunny said as we reached the bar, and she slipped the dirty glasses through an opening in the wall, presumably to a kitchen. "He's smarter than most give him credit for."

"Any tips?" Rylie asked while Bunny started pouring drinks. It was a wonder that she'd taken everyone's orders and remembered them while conversing with us.

"Know who you're looking for before you walk into a joint," Bunny said. "And try to be more inconspicuous next time."

"Next time?"

She shrugged and pointed at the empty seat where Arnie sat moments before. "Yeh let him get away."

17

"I still can't believe that old man was the bookie all along," Rylie said for the tenth time as we approached the O'Malley residences.

"Or was he?" I asked. "There's no way of knowing. Heck, maybe Bunny is the real mastermind. Did you see how she memorized all those drink orders while simultaneously talking to us?"

"You make a good point," Rylie said. "We should have gotten more information about Arnold from Brogan."

I was about to agree when I noticed Molly's official garda car in the driveway. At least, I assumed it was Molly's. My insides clenched. Was she here about the investigation, or had something else happened?

The driver stopped, but we didn't wait for him to come and let us out. Rylie pushed the door open, and we bolted up the stairs to the house.

It didn't take long to find Molly. She was in the sitting room with Gráinne and Donal, both of whom looked like they'd been crying.

"What happened?" I asked. "Where's Seamus?"

"Seamus is fine," Gráinne said with a sniffle.

"We've determined the cause of death in Sophie's case," Molly said.

"And?" Rylie and I said in unison.

"It was accidental. The horse likely spooked and threw her into the stall wall before trampling her."

I narrowed my eyes. "What brought you to that conclusion?"

"Not my conclusion," Molly said. "The medical examiner's. I'm just the messenger. Which means you need to stop going around telling people she was murdered."

"Did you tell her about the nail?" I asked Gráinne.

"As I told them, one nail in a horse stall is not enough evidence for us to conduct a murder investigation," Molly said.

I gaped at her. "The nail is completely different from what was used with Nuggie Buggie Boo-Boo Head. No other horses were in that stall. And the stall was cleaned out completely earlier that day."

"Let's just say that is enough to launch a murder investigation, how does that one nail bring us closer to the killer?" Molly's tone was more exhausted than condescending.

"Have you looked into Brogan?" Rylie asked, changing the subject. "He was in deep with some bookie at the Gaelic Gold Grotto."

"Arnold?" Molly asked weary laughter in her tone. "Have you met Arnold?"

Rylie put her hands on her hips. "Maybe you're underestimating him."

"Brogan had nothing to gain from Sophie's death," Molly said.

"But did he know that?" I asked. "Or did Arnold? Because, if not, they would have a motive."

"Lots of people have motives," Molly said. "That doesn't mean they are responsible. Sometimes, it's hard to face the facts because we don't want to believe what they tell us, but not everything is a murder investigation."

"Who else had the motive to kill my best friend?" Gráinne demanded.

When Molly didn't answer, I said, "Tilda, Vince, Wes."

"Yeh can't be serious thinking Wes had something to do with this," Seamus said from behind me.

"I don't think he killed Sophie, but he did go into the bar that night and announce to the crowd that he was responsible for her death," I said. "He likely meant it because he wasn't protecting her or something, but it's still possible. She had just broken up with him, and he's very knowledgeable about the stables."

"What about the farrier?" Seamus asked. "Has anyone spoken with him? He was supposed to be there that day, and we found the wrong nail. Maybe he had a beef with Sophie."

"He wasn't there," Gráinne said. "He was on vacation in Italy. I'd forgotten he sent a text postponing our standing appointment."

"Maybe another farrier?" Seamus asked, grasping at straws.

"As far as we're concerned, this was an accidental death," Molly said, starting toward the door. "And I'd suggest yeh take it as one, too, before someone files a complaint for harassment."

Rylie glared at her.

"If yeh have any more questions, feel free to call the station," Molly said.

"Hold on. I'll walk you to the door," I said.

Seamus had an angry look on his face when I walked toward him to meet up with Molly. He was probably furious that I'd thrown his friend under the bus. Of course, he was. I would be, too.

"I'm sorry I mentioned Wes," I whispered as I walked past.

Seamus shrugged but didn't look at me.

"Dinner's ready," Magella said, peeking her head in from the kitchen.

"I'll be right there," I said.

"What do yeh need, Shayla?" Molly asked her hand firmly on the door handle.

"I need you to take one more look at the autopsy," I said. "A closer one."

"I already—"

"Please," I said. "Look one more time. In the morning. With fresh eyes. If you look and don't find anything, I'll drop it."

"Yeh promise?"

I crossed my fingers behind my back and nodded.

"Yeh have yer fingers crossed, don't yeh?" Molly said with a sly grin. "Me daughter does that too."

"Just look. Please?"

"I'll see what I can do," she said. "No promises."

That was good enough for me.

Seamus didn't speak to me throughout dinner.

"The timing of the murder investigation getting called off was perfect since we have the dress appointment tomorrow," Gráinne said. "Unless you want me to reschedule?"

I'd completely forgotten about wedding dress shopping. "No need to cancel. I'm excited."

"Great," Gráinne clapped her hands together, smiling for the first time since the New Year's Day race. "The car will pick us up around ten."

"I never asked where we're going," I said. "Is there a wedding dress shop in Ballywick?"

"There's not," Gráinne said. "That's why we're going to Dublin."

Rylie squealed a bit in excitement. She hadn't seen much of Dublin since we'd picked her up at the airport and driven straight to the house.

As we finished our meal, Gráinne and Donal excused themselves from the table, leaving Seamus, Rylie, and me.

"Do yeh want an after-dinner drink?" Seamus asked.

Rylie and I both shook our heads.

"I'm good," Rylie said.

"Me too," I said. "I don't want any chance of a hangover tomorrow while shopping for a dress."

"Grand," Seamus said, plopping a kiss on the top of my head. "Then I'll be off to bed. See you when you come up."

He left the room without another word.

"He's really mad, isn't he?" Rylie asked.

"Seems that way," I said. "I should probably follow him upstairs so we can talk about it."

"I should probably turn in, too," Rylie said. "I'll need all the energy I can get for tomorrow's events."

As we approached the top of the stairs, ready to go our separate directions, Rylie turned and wrapped her arms around me.

"I'm sorry I got in the way today," she said.

I hugged her back. "No, I'm sorry. I was being so territorial about everything. I was just upset that you didn't seem that bummed about me moving here."

"Not that bummed?" Rylie pulled away, tears flooding her eyes. "I'm devastated. You're my best friend in the entire world. I've never had a friend like you. But I want you to be happy, and I can tell you're happy here."

A tear trickled down my cheek. "I am happy here, but I will miss you so much."

"We just have to make plans to see each other as much as possible," Rylie said. "Even if that means on FaceTime."

She took my hand, always the supportive friend despite her own feelings.

"Thank God for technology," I said, pulling her in for another hug. "And for best friends."

We stood there hugging and crying for quite some time before Rylie pulled away and said, "Now, go make up with your guy."

I smiled and turned away, but Rylie stopped me.

"Oh, and we're not stopping the investigation, right?"

"Nope. Not a chance," I said.

Rylie gave a nod. "That's what I thought."

18

It didn't take long for doubt to creep in. Was I making the right choice? Rylie had put on a brave face, but I knew this would crush her.

Still, the thought of leaving this new family I'd found was equally unbearable. Sure, Seamus would return to the States with me if that's what I wanted to do, but would he be happy there?

My heart ached for the loss either decision would bring. But Rylie was right—I was happy here. And we'd stay connected no matter what. I had to trust our friendship was strong enough to endure this.

When I walked in, Seamus was already tucked into bed, but he was still on his phone checking social media.

"Didn't expect yeh to come up so soon," Seamus said, setting his phone on the nightstand.

I changed into pajamas and slipped into bed. "I'm sorry I accused Wes."

"I understand. Yeh just don't know him like I do,"

Seamus said. "But he's a good friend of mine. I don't think he did anything to Sophie."

"You're probably right," I said. "And from what I know of him, I don't think he'd do it either."

"I'm sensing a but at the end of that statement."

I sucked in a breath, trying to figure out the best way to tell him what I was thinking. "But I know sometimes we do things when we're upset that we wouldn't normally do."

"I take it you're not giving up on the case?"

"No," I said. "Something tells me this wasn't an accident."

"Then I'll do everything I can to help clear Wes's name," Seamus said.

After a moment, I said, "I told Rylie."

"How did she take it?"

"Better than I expected," I said. "But it's still hard."

Seamus wrapped me in his strong arms. "I know this isn't easy, but it means the world that yeh've chosen a life here with me. We'll make sure you and Rylie stay close."

We were silent for quite a while before I got the nerve to bring up the money conversation. "Can I ask you a question?"

"Yeh just did."

I poked his side, and he squirmed a bit. "You know what I mean."

"Ask away."

My heart raced. "Do you want me to get a job?"

Seamus said nothing at first.

I sat up and looked back at him. "Because if you want

me to get a job, I will. I don't want to be a mooch. I'm not moving here or marrying you to be a kept woman."

Seamus finally broke into a smile. "Slow down there. Why do yeh think I think yer a mooch?"

"It's just that Sophie's husband was mooching off her, and I don't want you to think I'm doing the same."

"Come back down here." He pulled me to his chest and kissed my forehead. "I know yer not a mooch. Yeh didn't even know I had money until we arrived here. Yeh agreed to leave everything in America to come be with me."

"You're not answering the question," I said. "Do you think I should get a job?"

"Yeh already have a job."

"Hanging out with you is not a job." I laughed.

"Yeh do more than hang out with me," he said, his tone dead serious. "Yeh help me with the horses—the primary job in this family—and yer working on the castle renovations. Plus, yeh'll be planning the wedding and all that. If yeh want to get a job, I'm all for it, but yer not a mooch. My family and I are thrilled to spend money on yeh. Just ask me mam. She'll tell yeh straight."

Tears stung at my eyes as a lump formed in my throat. My entire childhood, I'd been told how expensive I was, how we couldn't afford new clothes or shoes. Everything was so different here. So much better.

"I love you," I said. "Thank you."

"Please never worry about money, okay? We have plenty of it."

We.

We felt nice.

The next morning, after a large breakfast, Magella, Gráinne, Rylie, and I left the house to find a posh black limousine waiting for us in the driveway. Gráinne wasted no time to pop the champagne and pour us all a glass.

"To new beginnings," Gráinne said, raising her glass for a toast. The clinking sound of glass sent tingles of excitement coursing through me.

Our journey took us past rolling green pastures that stretched endlessly. The road, a winding ribbon of pavement, meandered through small towns with charming stone cottages, ancient castles, and the occasional flock of sheep, causing a momentary traffic halt.

Gráinne, Rylie, Magella, and I took turns telling stories about life and love. Rylie and I stayed away from the topic of murder, which was quite the feat when we'd both been surrounded by it for so long.

The landscape gradually transitioned as we traveled eastward. Vast peat bogs and dense forests took center stage, interrupted only by serene lakes reflecting the ever-changing Irish sky. Sporadic signs pointing towards historic sites and cozy pubs dotted the route along the way, offering tempting diversions.

Rylie had a running list of places she wanted to see on a future trip typed into the notes app on her phone. Many of them were places I'd never heard of, but each time she mentioned one, Gráinne had a story about it. She'd been practically everywhere.

As Dublin neared, the open countryside gave way to more urbanized areas. The once-solitary road grew busier, flanked by modern houses, shopping centers, and the occasional industrial estate. The Dublin Mountains, a series of rolling hills, loomed in the distance, watching over the capital city.

"Wow," Rylie said, taking in the view.

I'd been to Dublin a handful of times, but it never got old. Driving into the city felt like a leap through time, with its blend of historic Georgian townhouses and innovative modern architecture.

The air seemed to pulse with energy as streets buzzed with pedestrians, from students to businesspeople, each absorbed in their own worlds.

"This is it," Gráinne said as we pulled up. The scent of roasted coffee from nearby cafes mixed with the distant sounds of traditional Irish music, creating a distinctly Dublin symphony.

Donovan and Dove was a quaint two-story boutique nestled between the city's buildings. It felt like something out of a vintage postcard with its large black sign spelling out the shop's name in elegant white letters—a beacon for brides-to-be. The expansive glass windows on the ground floor boasted stunning white dresses, each waiting patiently for its perfect bride.

Rylie clutched my arm with infectious excitement. "I love that one." She pointed at the silhouette in the far right window. "It would look amazing on you." If we were closer, I suspected she'd have her nose pushed up against the glass.

Her excitement was contagious. I couldn't help the giddiness that wanted to burst out in a squeal.

A doorman held the door for us as we walked in. I closed my eyes and inhaled the delicate fragrance of freshly cut roses, subtle undertones of lavender, and the faint aroma of aged wood from the store's original fittings.

"Gráinne, you made it," a vivacious woman with silver hair hurried to gather Gráinne in her arms. She wore a long, flowing skirt patterned with Celtic knots, paired with a ruffled blouse and a vintage brooch shaped like a Claddagh–hands, heart, and crown.

"This is Áine Donovan," Gráinne introduced her friend. "This is Shayla Murphy, Seamus's fiancée, and Rylie Cooper, Shayla's friend from America. You know Magella."

She kissed all three of us on each cheek. The smell of lavender and vanilla mixed with the old leather of books drifted off her in light waves.

"It's a pleasure to meet each of you," Áine said in a melodic voice. It was almost like wind chimes—delicate yet strong. "Especially you, Shayla. I've prepared a few gowns based on Gráinne's description, but I want you to pick out anything you like."

I hesitated. Did she mean I should go through all the beautiful gowns on the floor? They all looked so fancy and expensive. How would I choose one?

"Go now," she said. "Ciara will take any dresses you'd like to try on up to the loft, where we'll be waiting with champagne and snacks."

Gráinne, Magella, and Áine walked away, leaving Rylie and me to our own devices. I had no idea who Ciara was, but I assumed we'd eventually find out.

"Did Gráinne have the entire place closed down for you?" Rylie asked, pointing at the beautifully handwritten sign that read *Closed for a Private Party*.

I shrugged. "It's not all that surprising when you get to know Gráinne. She loves shopping and knows everyone." Gráinne would have also rearranged the stars for her loved ones if she could.

"How much do you think these gowns cost?" Rylie asked, looking for a price tag on one of the ones closest.

"The prices are not listed," a young woman in her early twenties, who I assumed was Ciara, said. "But don't worry, Gráinne has already clarified that money is no object."

I gaped at the raven-haired woman. This was already shaping up to be the most magical, memorable shopping trip of my life.

"If that's the case," Rylie said. "We'd like to try the one in the window. All the way in the corner. And this one, too."

She pointed at a dress that looked like it belonged on a Greek goddess that I'd have never chosen for myself. I reminded myself to keep an open mind. It wasn't like I'd known what I wanted to wear anyway, but the Greek goddess wasn't exactly it.

Slowly, though, I got into the action, adding a dress with an off-shoulder design, a deep V-neck, and sheer tulle. Another with a fitted bodice, a square neckline, and a tasteful V dipping down gently in the middle. I let my inner princess come out, imagining myself in the castle dancing the night away with Seamus as I chose lavish dresses I'd have never dreamed I could wear.

As Ciara took the last dress up the stairs, we followed.

It was surprising they didn't have an elevator, or if they did, they didn't use it. But Ciara seemed just as upbeat as ever when we reached the top. She wasn't even out of breath.

"You've chosen wisely," Áine said. "These are some of the finest gowns in all of Ireland. Possibly even the world."

Her words sent a flutter through my core. This was really happening.

Rylie joined me in the dressing room to help me zip and tie and button all the things I couldn't reach. I'd pulled my curls up into as elegant a bun as possible at the nape of my neck in what I expected to be the hairstyle I'd go with on my wedding day. I'd even put on more makeup than normal to get the full effect.

The first dress was too puffy, and the second was too itchy.

The third was the one Rylie had chosen from the window.

"I like it, but it seems a bit plain," I said, looking in the mirror. The design was undeniably sleek—a strapless, sweetheart neckline complemented the form-fitting silhouette that slightly flared at the bottom. But I couldn't help but feel it was a touch too understated for the occasion.

Rylie, however, was beaming at me. She clasped her hands together, her eyes practically glowing. "You look amazing. Come on, let's show the others."

We walked out to a chorus of oohs and ahs. Magella and Gráinne's eyes were practically heart-shaped.

I tried my hardest to smile, but I couldn't picture myself in this dress, standing in the middle of a castle to get married. It was beautiful but seemed more fit for a beach than a castle.

Áine, who had been through this before, chimed in, "I think it's beautiful, but there are so many more to try on. Let's keep going."

When I gave her a thankful smile, she winked at me.

The following two dresses were not at all what I wanted. One was the Greek goddess dress that looked more like I was going to a fraternity toga party than a wedding, and the other had a slit so high I'd have to be way too careful.

The next dress had looked promising on the mannequin. Its elegance had immediately captured my attention. The silky fabric glided over my skin as I slipped it over my head. The material caught the room's light in the mirror, giving it a subtle glow. My favorite part was the plunging back adorned with delicate buttons that trailed downwards, leading to a voluminous skirt and a moderately long train. It hugged my curves perfectly while allowing me to move freely.

The dress seemed to whisper of timeless beauty, its simplicity punctuated by those intricate details. Rylie buttoned each button carefully as I slid my hands down the soft material.

"Oh my gosh," I said with a little squeal. "It has pockets."

When Rylie finished buttoning, I stepped out of the dressing room and stood on the little podium in front of the mirrors.

The room was silent. I searched for expressions from Gráinne and Magella, but they seemed slightly shocked.

It wasn't until I caught Rylie's eye in the mirror that I realized they were in awe. She had her hands covering her mouth and tears in her eyes. Pure joy emanated from her.

As my gaze left Rylie and came to focus on my reflection, I knew. This was the dress.

I turned back to Gráinne and nodded.

She jumped from her seat and let out a loud whoop. "It's absolutely perfect!"

The room erupted in agreement.

Áine poured champagne, which I carefully took.

Ciara appeared with various options for headpieces and veils.

"Shayla," Gráinne said. "Can we hold off on the veils and such for now? I'd like yeh to look at a few things in my private collection first."

That was fine by me. I couldn't get the words out, so I just nodded.

She hugged me. "You look stunning."

"Should we eat now?" Magella asked. "I'm famished, and I didn't even try on all those dresses."

"Yes, absolutely," Gráinne said. "I'll finish everything up and meet yeh in the car."

"Thank you so much," I said. She'd insisted multiple times that she would pay for all aspects of the wedding. I'd fought her several times to no avail.

"It's the pleasure of me life to buy me children things," Gráinne said.

Tears welled in my eyes. With those words, any

lingering guilt about the expense was lifted. This was a gift from her heart.

"Don't cry on the dress, dear," Áine said.

19

Gráinne had made reservations at The Ivory Tower, one of Dublin's most exclusive restaurants. I'd never been anywhere so elegant.

The maître d' greeted us warmly. "Welcome, ladies. Please follow me."

We followed him up a grand staircase lined with fresh orchids and intricate iron railings. At the top, my breath caught as the dining area came into view. Towering ceilings soared above, trimmed in ornate crown molding. A massive chandelier glittered like a cascade of diamonds, casting a warm glow across the space.

Our table overlooked the bustling city below. I pressed my hands against the window, admiring the view. Twinkling lights from buildings and cars moved like shooting stars against the night sky.

"This is incredible," Rylie said, joining me.

"A special day requires a special end," Gráinne declared, settling into her chair.

A server arrived with menus bound in rich leather. As I

opened mine, the aroma of freshly baked bread wafted up, mingling with notes of fine leather and mahogany.

My eyes widened at the selections. Foie gras, seared scallops, braised short ribs—it was a food lover's paradise. After much debate, I decided on the pan-seared duck breast with a port wine reduction. Rylie chose the rack of lamb with roasted potatoes.

While we waited for our food, Gráinne ordered a bottle of champagne. The bubbly liquid energized us after our long day. We raised our glasses in a toast.

"To the future Mrs. O'Malley!" Rylie cheered.

I couldn't stop smiling. In just a few short months, I'd be walking down the aisle toward the man of my dreams.

"Have you decided on flowers?" Áine asked.

"I'm thinking white roses with touches of greenery," I replied. "And I'd love to incorporate some wildflowers from the countryside."

"Oooh, yes!" Rylie agreed. "That would be so beautiful and romantic."

We spent the next while discussing floral arrangements and other wedding details. Rylie eagerly made notes about ideas for my bachelorette party.

Our food arrived masterfully plated with artistic drizzles and garnishes. The duck practically melted on my tongue, perfectly complemented by the sweet tang of the sauce. Rylie closed her eyes as she savored the first juicy bite of lamb.

"I could get used to this," she joked.

As we neared the end of our meal, a commotion at the bar below caught my attention. A man and woman had cornered another gentleman, talking in hushed yet insistent tones. Something about the interaction gave me pause.

I recognized the woman's bright orange hair first. "Isn't that Bunny from the casino?"

"It is!" Rylie exclaimed. "What's she doing here?"

We watched the tense exchange continue. Though we couldn't hear what was being said, the body language spoke volumes. The man standing off to the side—who I now realized was Arnold—had an aggressive stance, gesturing angrily with his finger. The cornered man recoiled under the barrage.

"This doesn't look good," I said. "Should we do something?"

Gráinne's eyes narrowed. "I have a bad feeling about this. We should at least alert management."

Just then, Bunny grabbed the unknown man by his suit lapel, nearly lifting him off the ground. Arnold had to hold her arm to intervene.

The man pulled a wallet from his suit jacket and surrendered it. Arnold leafed through it, seeming to find what he wanted. He slipped something out before returning it.

"Did you see that?" Rylie asked. "Arnold took something from his wallet."

I nodded. "Cash, it looked like."

"They're shaking him down," Gráinne said.

Áine signaled for our server. "Could you please send the manager over? There's a disturbing situation unfolding near the bar that requires attention."

"Of course, right away." She hurried off.

We watched the manager descend the stairs and make

his way over. But by the time he arrived, Arnold, Bunny, and the other man had vanished. It was like they had disappeared into thin air.

The manager glanced around in confusion before returning upstairs. "My apologies. I don't see anything unusual at the moment."

"You just missed it," Rylie informed him. "Two people were harassing a man at the bar. They took his wallet and stole cash."

"Do you know who they were?" he asked, concerned.

We gave them Bunny's and Arnold's names and descriptions.

The manager shook his head. "I'm very sorry about this incident. Please let me know if you notice those individuals return. Rest assured, we do not tolerate such behavior at The Ivory Tower and will have them removed at once."

After he departed, an uneasy silence fell over our table. Our carefree wedding chatter had been replaced by something more sinister.

"There's still a possibility that those two had something to do with Sophie's murder," Rylie said. "Even if it's not probable."

"Come on, now," Gráinne said. "Sophie wouldn't want our evening ruined on account of those two."

She ordered a round of Irish coffees.

"You're right," Rylie said. "And you still haven't told me what you're doing for your honeymoon."

My honeymoon? I hadn't even considered a honeymoon. Everything was so perfect here. My entire life felt like a honeymoon. "I don't know. We still have to figure that out."

Our conversation drifted to ideas for the floral centerpieces and what music the band should play. Rylie's notes had expanded to multiple pages.

After dessert, we gathered our things to leave. The manager stopped by our table once more.

"Again, my sincerest apologies for the incident earlier," he said. "Please allow me to cover this evening's expenses."

Gráinne waved her hand. "That won't be necessary. We're just glad those crooks are no longer here causing trouble."

He nodded. "Understood. But if there is anything at all I can do to make up for it, don't hesitate to ask."

"Actually," Gráinne replied, "I'd love to book yer venue for the bridal shower."

The manager's face lit up. "It would be our honor! We can arrange the finest menu and wine pairings. When is the special date?"

After working out the details, he escorted us downstairs. The bar area was now bustling with well-dressed patrons enjoying evening cocktails. There was no trace of Arnold, Bunny, or the man they'd accosted earlier.

Outside, our limo driver opened the door, and we slid in. My feet ached from a full day, but my heart was full. Not even that unsettling scene could dampen my joy.

As Dublin's nighttime skyline receded into the distance, Rylie squeezed my hand. "This was the perfect ending to a perfect day."

I rested my head on her shoulder, completely content.

"It really was perfect. And soon, we'll be back here celebrating with everyone."

Gráinne raised a glass. "To the perfect wedding!"

"The perfect wedding!" we cheered. The sound echoed through the limo like music. In that moment, all was right with the world.

20

As we made our way up the driveway, a text came through on my phone. It was from the person I least expected—Molly.

MOLLY RYAN

It was murder. See autopsy photos attached. Heading to arrest Wes now.

I pulled up the photos she sent—one of the horseshoe marks on Sophie's face and the other of a horseshoe mark on Sophie's stomach.

I went back and forth between them until I realized—they weren't of the same horseshoe.

"Rylie," I said, shaking her gently to wake her. "Look at this."

Rylie's eyes fluttered open, and I handed her the phone.

"Flip through the pictures," I said.

She yawned and started swiping through. "What am I looking at?"

Magella and Gráinne sat in silence, but their attention was on us.

"Do you see the difference?" I asked. "The horseshoes."

Rylie gasped with realization. "Those are two different horseshoes."

I nodded. "Which means there had to be more to the story than just Boo-Boo trampling her."

"Can I see?" Gráinne asked.

I hesitated. "It's Sophie."

"I know," she said. "But maybe I can decipher the different horseshoes?"

"If you're sure," I said, holding the phone out for her.

Gráinne winced at the pictures, her eyes misting over. "Those are Boo-Boo's horseshoes." She pointed at the larger one that had a slightly odd shape. "But this one—this one has a brand on the end of the shoe. It's not our farrier's brand."

"Do you know whose it is?" I asked.

Gráinne nodded. "His name is Rian."

"We'll need to talk to him as soon as possible," I said. "She's on her way to arrest Wes right now."

"Wes? Why? Does she have evidence?"

"She'd have to have something to arrest him, wouldn't she?"

"I bet she heard about him spouting off in the pub," Rylie said. "We need to get to him before she does and see what he has to say."

"Agreed," I said.

Gráinne tapped on the window separating us from the driver. "Will you please take us to the stables?"

He turned down a different road than he would have to take us to the main house.

"We probably only have about five minutes before Molly arrives," I said as we got out of the car. "We have to make this quick."

Gainne, Magella, Rylie, and I all piled out and rushed to Wes's house. It was one of the biggest staff houses and closest to the stables.

"Hey Shayla, what's the craic?" Wes asked when he opened the door. "Oh, Mrs. O'Malley. Mags. Rylie. What are yeh all doing at me door?"

"We need to ask you some questions. We need the truth," I said. "And we have to make it quick."

"Why?"

"Molly's on her way to arrest you for Sophie's murder."

His face went pale. "Murder?"

"It wasn't an accident," Rylie said. "She was murdered. And you were at the pub telling everyone you were responsible."

"I thought I was," Wes said. "But not because I murdered her. We fought before she went in with Boo-Boo. I thought she might have been off her game or something."

"Were yeh really fighting about breaking up?" Gráinne asked.

Wes tilted his head back and looked up at the ceiling. "How'd yeh know about that?"

"You told us when you were drunk the other night," Rylie said.

"Gardaí will be here at any moment," I said. "If you don't tell us the truth, we can't find who did this."

His head jerked back down. "Yeh think yer gonna find her killer?"

"We're going to try," I said.

"Fine." He sucked in a breath. "We were arguing because she told me we had to stop seeing each other."

"Did Brogan threaten her?" I asked.

"Brogan?" Wes said with a laugh. "Sophie couldn't have cared less about Brogan. She'd already filed for divorce."

"Then why couldn't you be together?" Gráinne asked.

"Because she was about to be sued heavily. She suspected she'd lose everything, and she said she didn't want to take me down with her." Wes shook his head. "I'd have gone down with that ship any day. And I told her so. But she insisted. When we heard yeh hollerin' for us, we tabled the discussion, but I thought we'd be able to hash it out at a later date."

"Was Tilda the one suing her?" Gráinne asked.

"Dunno," Wes said. "She didn't tell me. I assumed so."

A thought popped into my head. "Do you know the code to Sophie's phone? Maybe if we can get into her email or texts, we can figure out if Tilda was suing her." Amongst other things.

"It's one, one, two, two, three, three," Wes said. "She changed it yesterday."

"Why?" I asked, pulling the phone out of my purse.

It was dead.

Of course.

"She changed it all the time. Probably to keep Brogan out."

"What about the power?" I asked. "Did you cut the power?"

"No one cut the power," Wes said. "The electric company said they thought we didn't pay our bill. They cut the power at midnight and didn't realize their mistake until later that morning."

"What about Rian—did yeh see him pokin' around at all?"

"Rian? As in the farrier?" Wes shook his head. "Nah. Never seen him 'round here."

"So, who would you think killed her if you had to guess?" I asked.

"Tilda," Wes said without hesitation

"She was out of town," I said. "At a race."

"Then she hired someone," he said. "I don't know."

The garda car came screaming up the driveway.

Molly stepped out and made a beeline for Wes.

As she arrested him, he pleaded for us to find out who did it.

21

Seamus and Donal arrived at the stables just as Molly was pulling away with Wes in the backseat of her car.

"They arrested Wes?" Donal said. "It can't be Wes."

"We don't think so either," I said.

Seamus walked up next to me and slid an arm around my back. "Do yeh know who did it?"

"Do you think the farrier—or *a* farrier—could have done it?" I asked. "I know Wes said he wasn't here, but with the two different horseshoe prints, it seems he might at least know something."

"Why would yeh think it's the farrier?" Donal asked.

"We found a silver nail in the stable when Boo-Boo's horseshoe nails are copper," Rylie said.

"And Molly sent over some photos that make it clear Sophie was hit with two different horseshoes." I pulled out my phone and let them each examine the photos.

"I'll call Rian and have him here first thing tomorrow morning," Gráinne said.

After saying goodnight to everyone, Seamus, Rylie, and I hurried back to the house, eager to charge Sophie's phone and see if it held any clues. I dug through my purse for my extra phone charger. Luckily, her phone was the same type as mine.

I plugged it in on the kitchen counter and waited anxiously as the screen flashed a low battery symbol.

"What do you think we'll find on it?" I asked Seamus and Rylie.

"Hopefully, something that will help us figure out who wanted to hurt her," Rylie said.

We watched as the seconds crawled by. The suspense was killing me.

Finally, the screen lit up, and I grabbed the phone. Swiping to unlock it, I held my breath. This was it.

I typed in one, one, two, two, three, three.

Sophie's home screen featured a picture of a horse. My heart squeezed thinking about how much she loved her job.

I opened her text messages first, scrolling through conversations with various people—her parents, clinic staff, Wes. Nothing jumped out as suspicious.

Next, I checked her call log. Most seemed like routine calls. All except one.

The day she died, she'd received a call from a restricted number that lasted over thirty minutes.

"That's odd," I said, showing Seamus and Rylie. "Any ideas who it could be from?"

Rylie shrugged.

"It looks like a local number," Seamus said. "Maybe we should call it back."

"Not on Sophie's phone," I said. "Maybe on one of our phones."

Seamus pulled out his phone and typed in the number before hitting the call button.

"Harry?" Seamus asked.

I gasped. From the pub?

"Hey, it's Seamus," Seamus said. "I just saw I got a call from this number and wanted to see who it was. Did yeh call me?"

Rylie and I waited, both of our breaths held.

"Oh, okay, right," Seamus said. "Thanks, Harry."

He hung up.

"So?" I asked.

"It's the public phone at the pub," Seamus said. "Yeh know, the one people used to call the cab or someone to pick them up?"

"So someone called Sophie from that phone right before she died," Rylie said.

"And they talked for a long time," I said. "Maybe Harry will remember who was on the phone that long."

Seamus shook his head. "I doubt it. It's not within view of the bar."

I pushed away the frustration and returned to Sophie's phone.

I clicked on her voicemail. There was only one from a few days prior. I put the phone on speaker so Seamus and Rylie could hear, too.

"Sophie, this is your mother. Your father and I think you should end things with that Wes fellow. Yes, we know about him. Brogan is beside himself with sadness. And he is your husband . . ." the voicemail went on.

I looked at the two sets of eyes fixed on me. "This doesn't help us. I was so sure we'd find something useful."

"Don't worry, we're making progress," Rylie said. "We'll figure it out."

By the following day, Gráinne had pulled together the staff for an impromptu tea and got the suspected farrier to agree to meet us under the pretenses of discussing his services.

"I may have made him think we were looking for a staffing change," she said. "I asked him to bring his portfolio."

The doorbell rang, and we all took our places.

"Hello," Gráinne said with a big smile on her face. "Thank yeh for coming on such short notice."

Rían practically bowed at the sight of her. I almost felt bad that he was getting his hopes up to work for the best in the business. My feelings quickly soured when I remembered he might have something to do with Sophie's death.

Gráinne, Rylie, and I went into the kitchen, where a beautiful tea service was set at the table in front of the fireplace.

"This looks lovely," Rían said. "You didn't have to do all this for me."

"It's my pleasure," Gráinne said. "Please, help yourself. I hope you don't mind. My future daughter-in-law and her friend are joining us."

"I'm Shayla, the future daughter-in-law." I shook his clammy hand.

"And I'm Rylie, her friend."

Rían reached into his large messenger bag and pulled out a binder. "This is my portfolio." His hand shook as he reached for one of the delicious-looking finger sandwiches.

Gráinne's smile faltered slightly when she opened the book.

I glanced over to see a horseshoe on the first page with a star engraved on the end.

"That's an interesting mark," I said. "Is the star something all farriers do?"

"We all have our trademarks," he said. "Mine is a star because my mom always told me I'd grow up to be a star."

"Cute," Rylie said.

"Did yeh bring a list of references?" Gráinne asked, pushing the book toward me and plastering a smile back on her face.

I couldn't imagine how hard it had to be to sit there and question someone about the murder of your best friend.

"O'course," he said, pulling a sheet of paper from his bag. "These are my most recent clients."

Gráinne turned the list so I could see. Tilda was number one on the list.

Goosebumps ran down my arms.

"I see you work with Tilda Williams," Gráinne said. "How has that been?"

"I prefer not to speak about my clients. Confidentiality and all."

"Of course, of course," Gráinne said. "I'd want confidentiality as well if I should hire yeh. I've just heard she's a challenge to work with."

"We can all be challenges at times, right?" Rian said with a shrug.

Gráinne wasn't getting anything from this line of questioning.

"How recently have you worked with Ms. Williams?" I asked.

He leaned toward her and whispered, "I traveled with her to the last two races, both of which her horses won in my shoes."

Gráinne's eyes lit up. "That's very good. Congratulations."

"Thank you," he said.

"You said yeh traveled with her. Does that mean actually with her or as in with her horses, or how does that work?" Gráinne asked. "I've used my farrier for so long. I fear we do things a bit backward. I wouldn't want to overstep in any way."

"I don't travel directly with any of my clients," Rian said. "Not that that's out of the realm of possibility if that's what you wanted. My clients typically have more important people to be around than their farrier."

"Did yeh see Tilda at both of the past two races?" Gráinne asked. "I hear she might have had some trouble getting to one."

He shook his head. "Not that I'm aware of. I believe she was there for both."

Gráinne nodded. "Obviously, I would worry that if yeh worked for the two of us simultaneously, there could be a conflict." Gráinne smiled sweetly. "Which is why I hire my farriers full-time, complete with room and board if they choose."

I could practically see dollar signs in his eyes.

"Though I quite understand if yer loyalties lie with Tilda. I'm sure she pays yeh handsomely for your services."

"Less than you'd think, honestly." He took another bite of the sandwich.

"Yeh said you shod both of the last two winners," Gráinne said. "I don't want any insider secrets—not that I'd understand them even if yeh told me—but what do yeh think made the difference?"

I had to keep myself from shaking my head. Gráinne knew the horse business inside and out. I was confident she'd understand anything Rían had to say.

"The shoes, definitely," Rían said, confidence in his voice. "They were a new kind I was trying—Tilda said to do whatever I needed to for the win."

"That's fantastic," Gráinne said. "Yeh must be devastated after all that work that you're not able to be in the winner's circle with Tilda and the jockey."

He glanced down. "I mean, a little recognition would be nice."

"By chance, did yeh shoe the horse who fell?" Gráinne asked.

His gaze popped back up to Gráinne. "I did, but I had nothing to do with the accident. I assure you, that horse has been sickly for weeks."

"Oh my," Gráinne said. "That's horrible. I'm shocked Sophie allowed it to race at all."

"She didn't want it to," Rían said. "But Tilda insisted. Sophie quit right after that race."

"And then she died," Gráinne said.

"She died here, right?" Rían said.

Gráinne nodded, tears coming quickly to her eyes. "Boo-Boo trampled her."

"The horse who won on New Year's Day?" Rían said.

"That's the one." Gráinne wiped the tears from her eyes. "I just can't bring myself to go to any races after what he did."

"Surely you have a backup horse."

"Bubba Bagooshka isn't quite ready to race."

"That's too bad." He shifted in his seat like a child, waiting for the perfect moment to ask for a piece of candy. "What will you do with Boo-Boo?"

"I'll sell him, I suppose," Gráinne said.

"But he's a sure winner," Rían said. "People would pay top dollar, and you'd essentially be selling away your victories."

"He killed my best friend," Gráinne said. "I have no use for a horse who would do such a thing."

"Horses are fickle," Rían said. "Maybe his shoes were on wrong, or something spooked him. I could work with him. I could do so many things to help him be the best."

"Did you like Sophie?" Gráinne asked, her voice still filled with emotion.

"Everyone liked Sophie," he said. "She was a gem. And she cared about the horses above all else. You know? I was so shocked when I heard she'd been trampled to death. I know Boo-Boo is easily spooked, but I never saw her with a horse who didn't adore her."

"Boo-Boo loved her, too. Until he turned on her." Gráinne slammed her fist on the table for effect, making all three of us jump in our seats. "I'm sorry. My emotions sometimes get the better of me."

"Maybe he didn't trample her on purpose—maybe someone spooked him so he'd do it."

Gráinne narrowed her eyes at him. "Are you implying someone might have murdered Sophie?"

"It's possible," he said. "And likely more probable than Boo-Boo turning on her."

"If yeh had to guess who would want Sophie dead, who would yeh guess?" Gráinne stared at him as he squirmed in his chair.

"I—uh—well." He looked like a wild animal backed in a corner. If he mentioned his current client, he could be out of a job, but if he didn't answer, Gráinne might not hire him.

He finally spoke. "The only person I know who had a problem with Sophie was Tilda."

22

We didn't get much more out of him after he threw suspicion on his boss. Gráinne told him she'd call him after she thought about it. From the look on his face, he knew he wasn't getting the job.

"Back at the beginning with Tilda," I said as Gráinne, Rylie, and I returned to the sitting room.

"How can we corroborate the fact that she was at that race?" Rylie asked. "Surely people saw her, right?"

"If Molly suspected Tilda, she could probably find out if there were airplane records or money transfers that might have implied she paid someone to do it." I pulled out my phone and sent her a quick text message. When she didn't reply after a few seconds, I slipped it back into my pocket.

Gráinne turned on the TV, and Tilda's face appeared on the screen.

We let out a collective groan.

"This is the third race in as many days you've won.

How does it feel?" the announcer asked.

As she replied, they played a montage of the three wins, all by the same horse. "It feels like a dream come true. My entire life, I've been working toward this."

"Wait, is that who I think it is?" I asked as a man in a cowboy hat laid a big fat kiss on Tilda in one of the clips.

"Doesn't surprise me they're together," Gráinne said. "They're perfect for each other."

"Right, but he's been trying to buy Boo-Boo. Like, really trying, right?"

"He's called me multiple times a day about it," Gráinne said. "I finally had to have Seamus show me how to block a phone number."

"And he admitted he wants to buy the horse for Tilda—or at least that's what he wants us to believe," I said.

Rylie looked confused.

"What if either he or Tilda or both of them want to buy Boo-Boo because of some sort of evidence the police might get off Boo-Boo?" I asked. "Like, what if they gave him something to make him go crazy or something?"

"It's not altogether unreasonable to think that," Rylie said.

"Especially since Tilda already has a winning horse," Gráinne said.

"We need to get someone to take Boo-Boo's blood immediately," I said.

"I'll just call So—" Gráinne started but stopped herself. "I mean, I'll call someone from Sophie's clinic. I'm sure there's someone there who can do a simple blood draw and test."

My heart broke at the look on Gráinne's face. The

minute she remembered she couldn't just pick up the phone and call Sophie, her entire body seemed to crash into a metaphorical brick wall of sadness.

"I can make the call," I said.

"Oh, don't be silly," Gráinne said, trying to smile through the crack in her voice. "It's all right."

While she stepped out of the room to make the call, Rylie turned to me. "Even if Tilda was at the race that day, Vince might not have been. He could have easily taken some other horse's horseshoes, put them on the bottom of his boots, and stomped on Sophie after knocking her unconscious to make it look like the horse did it."

Before I could acknowledge the thought, Gráinne came back into the room in a huff. "Yer not going to believe this."

"What?" I asked.

"Sophie's parents already sold her practice to Doctor Collins."

I gasped. "No."

"Yes," she said. "They signed the papers this morning. The woman on the phone was distraught. They're firing a bunch of staff."

"Why would they do that?" I asked.

"He was willing to pay a hefty price, and he's the only other vet in the area who deals with the scope of animals that Sophie used to."

"Did they need the money?" Rylie asked.

Gráinne shook her head. "Not in the slightest."

"Should we call a vet from a town over?" I asked.

"Yes," Gráinne said. "Donal would never forgive me if I let Collins care for our horses. I need to move our entire account right away. I don't want Collins to have access to our records."

"You take care of that," I said. "We'll head out to the barn and see what we can find with Boo-Boo."

"Just make sure someone goes in with you," Gráinne said. "I'd never forgive myself if something happened to yeh in there."

Gráinne hurried out, already on the phone, calling a car.

"Do you think there's evidence still on Boo-Boo?" Rylie asked.

"Probably not on his person—er, animal? Whatever. You know what I mean. But it doesn't hurt to check."

On our ride down to the stables, we passed Wes's house, where Molly stood outside amid several garda cars. I hit the brakes and nearly sent Rylie flying into the windshield.

"Sorry," I said.

She waved me off. "What are they doing here?"

Molly must have overheard her because she turned. When her gaze caught mine, she sighed, her shoulders slumping.

"What's going on?" I asked her.

"We found items in Wes's house that implicate him in Sophie's murder," she said.

"What kind of things?" I asked.

"That's garda business." Molly didn't sound completely stern on that point.

"If I hadn't told you to look at that autopsy photo more closely, you wouldn't have even known this was a murder," I said.

"And for that, I thank you," she replied. "And offer an apology for brushing you off at the beginning of all this."

"Then you owe it to me to tell me what you found in his house," I said. "I know you didn't find horseshoes that match the prints left on Sophie's body—the ones with the stars. Those came from a farrier that has never visited this place until today."

Molly's smile tightened, and her voice dropped to a whisper. "I can't tell yeh what I found. Yer too close to all this. And yeh need to stay out of it."

"I'll show you pictures of the crime scene if you tell me what you found," I said.

Her eyes widened. "Yeh took photos of the crime scene? When?"

"The night it happened. Right after we found Sophie."

Molly looked torn. The photos, since I took them with my camera phone, wouldn't hold as much weight in court as they would have if one of the garda officers had taken them, but they still had possible information that could help the investigation.

Which reminded me to look at them harder, too.

"Fine," she said. "But don't be telling anyone. Not Seamus, not Gráinne, and not Donal."

I started to cross my fingers behind my back, but Molly said, "And show me yer hands."

"I can't keep something from Seamus. It just isn't how we operate." The words slipped out of my mouth before I realized they might have been a dig at the relationship she and Seamus once shared.

"Seamus adores Wes," she said. "He could mess something up in the investigation if yeh tell him what I'm about to tell yeh."

"I'll do my best not to tell him," I said. "Now, do you want the pictures or not?"

She shifted her weight from one foot to the other, taking one more glance behind her to ensure no one was watching us. "We found a box of horseshoes stuffed inside a dirty laundry bin. The horseshoes were the same ones as what we believe struck Sophie."

"Not possible," I said. "Someone has to be setting him up."

"That's not all," Molly said. "We also found performance-enhancing drugs in his kitchen."

Warmth started up my neck. "What do you mean, performance-enhancing drugs?" I lowered my voice barely above a whisper. "Like for men? In the bedroom?"

It was Molly's turn to be embarrassed. "No!" She looked around to make sure no one had turned because of her outburst. "Not for humans. For horses."

Things started clicking into place. Maybe he and Sophie had been arguing about a care plan after all. Maybe he'd lied about them breaking up. Had she discovered him drugging the horses and threatened to come out with the information?

"Gráinne needs to know about this," I said. "If this gets out, every one of her wins will be overturned."

"Don't they take blood tests on the horses after races?" Rylie asked.

"I guess I don't know," I said. "Maybe they do—"

The rest of my sentence was cut off by the sound of a truck pulling a horse trailer driving past. When it was gone, I continued. "If they do, then Gráinne would be in the clear."

"Either way, yeh can't tell her. Not yet. This is massively confidential." Molly crossed her arms over her chest. "Can I see the pictures now?"

I opened my phone and scrolled past the photos of the wedding gowns and selfies with Rylie, Gráinne, and Magella. The crime scene photos were hard to look at, with Sophie lying dead in many of them.

Molly studied them closely. Did they tell a story? And if so, was it that Wes had killed Sophie?

Finally, Molly handed my phone back. "Can yeh send them to me?"

I tapped my screen a few times. "Done."

Molly lifted her phone, waiting for the message to come through. When it did, she returned it to her pocket. "Thanks."

"It looks bad, but it couldn't have been Wes," I said. "Have you looked into Tilda? They did take blood from the horse that fell in the last race. Maybe she planted this here to make Wes and Sophie look bad."

"Tilda has been out of the country almost entirely since New Year's Day," Molly said. "She has a solid alibi."

"Then maybe she hired someone to do her dirty work," Rylie said. "What about Vince? He's slimy."

"Vince who?" Molly asked.

"Tilda's boyfriend. The horse buyer from Texas," I said. "He's been practically begging to buy Boo-Boo since—" The thought caught in my mind. He'd wanted to buy Boo-Boo for Tilda since the day of the race. Before Sophie's murder.

"Since when?" Molly asked, waiting for me to finish my sentence.

"Since New Year's Day," I said.

Rylie's posture drooped a bit. She'd just realized the same thing.

"And what does that have to do with Sophie's death?" Molly asked.

"I don't know," I said. "Maybe I'm grasping at straws. But there's something not quite right about all this. And Wes definitely didn't do it. He loved Sophie."

Molly didn't reply.

When we'd stood in silence long enough, I said, "We're heading to the barn. Good luck finding the *actual* killer."

"Stay out of trouble," Molly said. "And out of the investigation. I should have listened to yeh before, but now it's personal. Yer judgment will be clouded."

I threw up a hand in a wave and slid into the driver's seat of the golf cart.

"He wasn't trying to buy Boo-Boo because there might have been evidence on Boo-Boo," Rylie said when we were far enough away from Molly.

"Not initially," I said. "But maybe he was afterward."

Rylie didn't reply, but from the dreary look on her face, I could tell she wasn't completely certain about that.

And now Gráinne was trying to get someone out to blood test Boo-Boo. If they found performance-enhancing drugs in his system, Gráinne could be ruined. Did they have a duty to report such things?

I picked up the phone and called Gráinne, but she didn't answer.

"I need to get her to stop that blood test," I said. "She has no idea what she might be walking into."

Rylie picked at her cuticles. "Try her again?"

I did, but still no answer. Then I called Seamus.

"Hello, Love."

"Hey," I said. "Have you heard from your mom? She was trying to find a vet to take some blood from Boo-Boo."

"Oh yeah, she told me about that. She called around but couldn't get anyone to come right away."

I let out a sigh of relief.

"Can you tell her not to let anyone take his blood?"

"Why not?"

"I can't tell you that," I said. "But it's important."

"I can try to call her, but she rarely answers when she's driving."

"Where is she driving to?" I asked. Maybe she had a lead on something else that would help solve Sophie's case.

"Well, she couldn't get anyone to come out, so she took Boo-Boo to the vet herself."

The truck and horse trailer that had gone by us before had been Gráinne with Boo-Boo?

I slammed on the brakes.

Thankfully, this time, Rylie was ready and held on. Gráinne probably didn't stop to chat with us because Molly was standing right there.

"What vet?" I asked, turning that cart around to head back to the houses. "We need to stop her."

"Yer freaking me out," Seamus said. "What's she gonna find?"

"I can't tell you," I said. "Molly made me promise."

"So it has something to do with the case. And Wes," Seamus said. He may not have dealt with all the same things as a park ranger as police officers did, but he was a smart cookie. "Did they find something at Wes's house?"

"Yes," I said.

"Something that makes him look guilty."

"Completely guilty. Plus some."

"Drugs?" Seamus's voice rose with surprise as the thought dawned on him. "Did they find drugs in his house? Horse drugs? No. That couldn't be it. He'd have never drugged the horses."

I didn't reply.

He let out a curse. "That's what they found, isn't it?"

"Among other things," I said. "I think he's being set up. Did the cameras come back online when the power came back? We need to see if anyone snuck into Wes's house and planted these items."

Seamus groaned. "I'll check."

"I don't think Wes did this," I said. "But if they find what I think they might find in Boo-Boo's blood, it could do real damage to the business's reputation."

"I'll check the cameras and try to get in touch with Mam," Seamus said.

"I think we need to talk to Sophie's colleagues at the vet's office before they're all gone," I said. "Rylie and I will head that way."

"Be careful, Love," Seamus said. "If there's a murderer out there willing to go to these lengths, who knows what else they'll do?"

23

The car glided along winding roads that sliced through the countryside's patchwork of fields. We passed charming cottages with empty flower boxes and an ancient castle blanketed in ivy.

As I drove up the winding road, the sprawling expanse of the Irish land was covered in a moody ambiance. The overcast sky painted everything in muted tones, but ahead, Sophie's vet office stood out with an undeniable touch of class.

This was no ordinary facility. Nestled amidst stretches of green, the stone façade of the building gleamed with an understated elegance, bearing the weight of meticulous craftsmanship. The architectural details hinted at both heritage and modernity—at a place where tradition met top-tier service.

Mature trees punctuated the manicured grounds, their branches swaying gently in the wind, casting fleeting shadows on the building. A spacious car park was dotted with high-end vehicles. Even the signage exuded a sense of luxury with its sophisticated font and subtle gold accents.

It was no wonder Brogan was so mad that Sophie hadn't left any of this to him. It was probably worth a fortune.

We parked next to a BMW and got out.

"This place is so fancy," Rylie said, awe tinging her voice.

"I guess if you're going to have high-paying clients, you have to have a high-class facility."

The faint antiseptic scent mingled with lavender and wood polish as I pushed open the heavy wooden door. Framed photos of champion horses covered the walls, paying homage to Sophie's life passion. Two women occupied the front desk, both wearing the same uncertain expression upon our entry.

The interior looked completely renovated with state-of-the-art everything.

"Can I help you with something?" the woman with a high brown ponytail and dark eyeliner asked.

"We'd like to speak to someone about Sophie," I said.

"Yer the ones trying to figure out who killed her, aren't yeh?" an older woman in a plaid button-down shirt asked, her voice hushed.

"That we are," I said.

"We can't tell you anything," the woman with the ponytail said, cutting a glance at the older woman. "We're under strict confidentiality agreements with the new owner."

"Is there anyone here who can talk to us about Sophie?"

"No," a tiny blonde woman said as she entered a doorway that presumably led to the back of the building.

Her white coat had her name embroidered on it—Lila James DVM.

"What does DVM mean?" I asked, pointing to her coat.

"Doctor of Veterinary Medicine," Lila said. "It means I'm a licensed veterinarian."

"Did you work with Sophie?"

"Yes," she said. "Sophie was my mentor."

"Don't you want justice for her?" Rylie asked.

"They've arrested someone," Lila said. "That sounds like justice to me. Now, if you need anything veterinary-related, we can help. If you need more information about Sophie, we can't discuss that *here*, and you're welcome to leave."

Neither of the two women at the desk seemed to notice how she'd placed inflection on the word here, but something told me she might talk to us elsewhere.

"Do you do house calls?" I asked. "I'm engaged to Seamus O'Malley."

This got the two women's attention.

"Gráinne has already fired us. Donal retrieved all of their files this morning," the woman with the ponytail said.

"Oh, right, because Doctor Collins bought the place?" I asked.

"That's correct," the ponytail woman said. "And to stay employed here, we've all signed non-disclosure agreements about anything and everything having to do with Sophie and the business she ran."

"Hmmm," I said, trying to figure out how to get Lila

away from the place to meet with us. I didn't want to sit in the parking lot waiting for her to leave work. That would likely get us turned in to the Guardaí, and that's the last thing we needed right now. "Well, I suppose we should just cut our losses and head to Harry's pub."

Rylie nodded. "Harry's Pub is a great place to meet friends."

The woman in the ponytail didn't hide her irritation with us, but Lila smiled from behind them and nodded slightly when they weren't looking.

It was only mid-afternoon, so it was possible that we'd be waiting a while before Lila could join us, but I'd be willing to wait.

"She knows something," I said to Rylie when we were back in the car.

"She definitely knows something," Rylie said.

"And she wants to tell us, even with a non-disclosure."

Rylie laughed. "You know, when you told me about Ireland, I had no idea it was actually as beautiful as you made it out to be. And the people are such characters. I can definitely see why you'd want to stay."

"You wouldn't want to move here with me, would you?" I asked, then quickly added, "I'm not serious. I know you never could, and that's so selfish of me."

Rylie pressed her lips together tight and wrinkled her nose.

"I know, I know," I said. "Pretend I never asked."

"Don't think I haven't thought about it," Rylie said. "I just don't know what I'd do here. I couldn't live with you guys—I mean, I know I could, but I'd want my own place, you know? And you and Seamus have a lot going on with the horses and the castle—which you still need to show me—and making a house for yourselves. I assume that's what the cottage is? Your house?"

She was so perceptive sometimes. "How'd you figure it out?"

"You're not hard to read, Shay," she said gently. "Every time we drive by or walk by, you smile at it like it's a long-lost friend. Honestly, if it wasn't a house, I'd be jealous."

"Alabaster left it for us in his will," I said. "I mean, he left us more than just the house, and then Killian threw a fit and gave up all his inheritance. And with Aoife in jail, we got hers too. So we basically ended up with everything set aside for the nieces and nephews."

"But Clara got everything else, right? Like the money and stuff?"

"Clara and Magella," I said. Clara was Magella and Alabaster's daughter, though she didn't know that as they'd never told her.

"I love a good rags to riches story," she said. "Not that Clara and Magella were in rags, but you know what I mean."

"It was amazing to see her stand up to Killian," I said. "He was being so awful about it."

"It sounds like he has some growing up to do."

"That's for sure."

Harry's was relatively dead this time of the afternoon.

We had no trouble finding a booth in a corner where Lila could stay unseen.

"What's the craic?" Harry asked. "I hear Wes was hauled off by the guards."

"You heard right," I said. "What else have you heard?"

"I hear lots of things," Harry said.

"About Sophie's death?"

He put a finger to his lips and tilted his head as if deep in thought. "Her parents sold her business and gave all the money to Brogan."

"What?" Rylie and I both practically shouted.

"Aye, keep it down, will yeh," Harry said. "Not that it's a secret, but it's not necessarily public knowledge."

"Why'd they do that?" I asked.

"He had some dirt on 'em. They didn't want to tarnish their good name. So they gave him what any normal husband would have gotten in the event of his wife's death. From what I hear, it was one less headache for them."

"And now his debts are paid," I said.

"Won't be for long," Harry said. "He's got an addiction, that one. Even with all the money they got on the business, he'll be out of it eventually."

"What do you know about Doctor Collins?" I asked. "The veterinarian who bought Sophie's clinic."

"Only what I hear around the pub," he said. "He's never been in for a pint."

That was weird. Everyone's been to Harry's.

"What have you heard?" Rylie asked.

"He likes to dabble in curses," Harry said. "Probably good he doesn't come around."

"How is he with the animals?" I asked.

Harry shook his head. "No idea. Don't have any animals meself. No time for 'em with the pub. Tried to have a cat once. Kept knocking pints off the bar into people's laps. Had to re-home him."

"If you hear anything else, will you tell us?" I asked. "About Collins or anything with Sophie?"

"If it be relevant, I will." Harry gave us a nod. "Now, what can I be gettin' yeh to drink?"

We each ordered a pint of the black stuff, and he ambled off to get it for us.

"What do you think about Brogan being a suspect?" Rylie asked.

"I don't know that Brogan thinks that far ahead," I said. "It's still possible that someone killed her, thinking Brogan would get money to pay them off, but honestly, that seems far-fetched, too. I mean, who's to say he'd have paid his debts with the money?"

"But he did pay them with the money he got from Sophie's parents," Rylie said.

"Probably because he's scared," I said. "If he thinks Arnold or one of Arnold's people killed Sophie to get money out of him, he'd definitely want that taken care of."

"Valid point."

"Let's set up a timeline," I said, pulling a notebook and pen from my purse. "I think if it's all on paper, we might be able to see the bigger picture."

Rylie wiggled in her seat. "Good idea."

"So we'll start at the race on New Year's Day. Sophie and Tilda got into an argument after Sophie saved Tilda's horse."

I wrote *New Year's Day* on the left and *Sophie*, *Tilda*, *Vince*, *Brogan*, and *Wes* at the top to start columns.

"We know Sophie, Tilda, and Vince were at the race. I suspect Brogan and Wes were not."

"Okay, then go to that night," Rylie said. "Brogan was

with his mistress, and Wes and Sophie were possibly together."

"Tilda was supposed to be leaving the country for the next race," I said. "And we have no idea where Vince was."

"The power goes out at midnight," Rylie said. "And we end up riding later that afternoon."

I added a column that said races at the top and opened my phone to an internet browser. "We need to know exactly when each race took place that Tilda was apparently at."

It wasn't hard to figure out. Tilda had it all listed on her website. I added them to the column.

"So the race the next day was in Northern Ireland?" Rylie asked.

"It's technically another country, but only about three to four hours away, depending on where the race was," I said. "And that's by car. By plane, it would have been even quicker. Probably less than an hour."

"Which would make it easy for her to hop on a plane, kill Sophie, hop on another plane, and get back in time for the winner's circle," Rylie said. "Wow. And Molly isn't even considering this?"

I shook my head. How could she not be considering this? Of course, she had found damning evidence in Wes's house, but that could have easily been planted there. I switched over to my text app and sent Molly a quick text.

> Were there fingerprints on the horseshoes or the drug bottles?

Her response came almost immediately.

> That's none of your business. Stay out of the case.

Then my phone rang from a number I didn't recognize. "Hello?"

"Seriously? Don't text me questions like that. My phone could be subpoenaed."

"Hello to you too," I said to Molly.

"No."

"Okay, no hello."

"I mean, the answer is no."

My heart felt like it jumped into my throat. "There were no fingerprints?"

She didn't reply. When I looked at my phone, the call had been disconnected.

"There weren't fingerprints on anything," I told Rylie. "He's being set up."

24

Once Rylie and I had fully written out the entire timeline, it seemed like any of them could have done it. Wes was on the property and had just fought with Sophie, Tilda could have easily gotten a flight, neither of us remembered if Vince was in the winner's circle with Tilda at the race that day, and Brogan was wholly unreliable.

"I really thought that would help us more," I said, slipping the notebook back into my purse.

"It's kind of like those murder boards you see in movies," Rylie said. "They never make any sense to me. Like, how can you even piece together a puzzle like that?"

"Didn't you have a case with a murder board once or twice?" I asked.

"Yeah, but it still didn't make all that much sense." Rylie's gaze stopped at something over my shoulder.

I turned to find who I thought was Lila walking toward us with a hood up and dark sunglasses covering her eyes.

I stood and let her slip into the booth so her back

would be to the door, and she'd be most hidden, then sat back down next to her.

"I have to make this quick because I could lose my job for this," she said. "And if I lose this job, I'll be blacklisted in the entire veterinary community. Not to mention cursed by our new leader."

I couldn't believe all these people thought Dr. Collins would curse them. But maybe he could. Who was I to judge?

"Tilda was giving her horses performance-enhancing drugs. Sophie caught her the day of the New Year's Day race," Lila said, slipping a folder out of her jacket. "This is proof. It has all the drug information and Sophie's notes. When she signed off on No-Name Jack's papers before that race, she told Tilda not to give the horse anything. No-Name Jack had several conditions—ones that didn't make him ineligible to race. But, let's just say, if Gráinne had faced the same prognosis on one of her horses, that horse would have lived the rest of its life grazing in her beautiful pasture."

"I'm guessing Tilda didn't take Sophie's advice?" I asked.

"That's correct," Lila said. "Right after Sophie signed the papers, Tilda fired her, then administered the drug."

"What did Sophie do?" Rylie asked.

"She tried to turn Tilda into the officials, but they simply said they'd test the winner for drugs after the race. Sophie knew it could kill the horse."

I nodded. "And it almost did."

"It would have if Sophie hadn't known what Tilda did," Lila said. "If anyone killed Sophie, it was Tilda."

"Did Tilda get blood testing done on No-Name Jack after the race?" I asked.

"It's likely," Lila said. "But there's no way she would have shared the results with Sophie. So Sophie decided to turn Tilda in to the authorities when Tilda got back from the next race. She told me everything over the phone but made me promise not to let anyone know I knew."

"Because if you did, you might be in danger, too," I said.

"Exactly," Lila said. "I turned the evidence that Sophie had on her computer over to the authorities the day after she died, right before they sold the business. They said they'd look into it, but I haven't heard back."

"And since then, Tilda's horses have been winning everything," Rylie said. "Do they drug test the winners?"

"The drugs Tilda's using are untraceable by the regular tests," Lila said. "They'd have to test for this specific drug."

"Then what evidence did you have?" I asked.

"Pictures of Tilda administering drugs with a time stamp for right before the race when No-Name Jack died," Lila said. "It's pretty damning evidence."

"Do you think it'll be enough?" Rylie asked.

"Only time will tell," Lila said. "Is there anything else you need from me?"

A thought popped into my mind. "Would there be any reason Sophie would have carried a plastic bag with her in her vet bag?"

Lila recoiled in horror. "Absolutely not. Plastic bags to horses are the equivalent of spiders or public speaking to humans. They're the scariest thing out there."

"So if we told you we found one in her vet bag right after she died?" I asked.

"I'd tell you someone planted it there," Lila said.

"And what about Wes?" I asked. "Do you know if he had given any of Gráinne's horses the drugs?"

"Absolutely not," Lila said, horrified. "Gráinne would have never stood for it."

"Maybe she didn't know?" Rylie suggested.

"Gráinne knows everything about those horses. Sophie tested their blood more than any other horses in her care. Gráinne is meticulous about her horses' health." She pulled the hood tighter around her face. "I should go. Be careful if you're planning to go up against Tilda. She's a right terror, that one."

Rylie and I finished our drinks and headed back to the house.

"I want to see if Vince is in the winner's circle with Tilda at that race," I said. "If not, he could have done her dirty work."

"And you're certain the times line up with the winner's circle and the time Sophie died?" Rylie asked.

"We were on the ride for about two hours," I said. "Give or take. The winner's circle moment would have happened sometime within those two hours."

"Which means, since Tilda was there, she has a solid alibi."

"Right, but if Vince isn't, he could have done it."

"It'll be hard to prove it if that's the case," Rylie said.

"It'll be far easier to prove that Wes did it with all the evidence in his house."

"Speaking of evidence in his house, we need to see if Seamus could pull up the camera footage, too."

"And if he got in contact with Gráinne."

My mind whirled a mile a minute. There were so many loose ends, but they all seemed to lead back to Tilda. At least, I hoped they did.

The house seemed completely empty when we got there. Even Magella wasn't there cooking or tidying.

"This house could definitely be creepy if it wanted to be," Rylie said.

"Especially with the hidden passageways," I said, wiggling my eyebrows. "I'll show you when this case is finished."

I pulled up the footage that Gráinne had recorded from the races. It looked like she hadn't watched any of them. Worry crept into my chest. Would she ever be the same after what happened to Sophie? Would she be able to continue with the horse racing business?

"You good?" Rylie asked.

"I just keep going back to how crappy it is that Gráinne lost Sophie. How hard that must be."

"I guess there are worse things than your best friend moving across an ocean," Rylie said with a small smile.

"Definitely," I agreed. "Okay, this is the race. Let's fast forward to the end, where they interview the jockey and the owner in the winner's circle."

I stopped at the end of the race. The powerful figure of Tilda's winning horse dominated the screen. Glistening beads of sweat clung to its sleek coat, its flaring nostrils exhaled mists of breath, and its eyes shimmered with a mix of exhaustion and triumph. And perhaps drugs?

The camera panned over its muscles, each ripple telling a story of determination and grace. As the lens slowly zoomed out, the jockey came into view. Dressed in vibrant colors, he was beaming, fatigue forgotten in the glow of victory. His gloved hands affectionately patted the horse's neck, and he beamed with pride.

Rylie and I were both on the edge of our seats.

Gradually, the full spectacle of the winner's circle unfolded. Proud team members and trainers converged, their faces bright with elation. The vibrant green of the turf served as a stark contrast to the rich browns and golds of the winner's garlands, which were being draped over the horse's withers. Off to the side, a grand silver trophy caught the gleam of camera lights, waiting for its moment in the limelight.

"Come on, keep going," Rylie said, impatience in her voice.

The camera then panned wider, capturing the ecstatic crowd surrounding the circle. Fans waved their betting slips and programs in jubilation. Flashes from photographers' cameras punctuated the scene like stars, eager to immortalize the moment of sporting glory.

"Did you see her?" I asked as the camera zoomed out farther to show the looming grandstands.

"I didn't," Rylie said. "But there were a lot of people. Let's watch it again."

We watched a second time but still didn't see her.

"What about Vince?" I asked.

"I don't see him either," Rylie said. "Keep going. Maybe they'll do the interviews."

We watched to the very end. The jockey was interviewed, a trainer was interviewed, even a spectator was interviewed.

Tilda wasn't interviewed—wasn't even mentioned.

"Was she even there?" I asked. "Does she even own the horse?"

"Let's not get ahead of ourselves," Rylie said. "Does she ever talk to reporters at the end of races? They didn't mention anyone else owning the horse, either."

"Yes, she has," I said. "Remember that footage from one of the more recent races on the news? She was talking right into the microphone."

"Then that solves it," Rylie said. "Tilda killed Sophie and probably had Vince's help to do it."

"Now, we just have to prove it beyond a reasonable doubt."

Returning to Tilda's race schedule, it looked like she'd be in Ballywick tomorrow afternoon, meaning we only had so much time to dig.

Seamus and Gráinne got home not long after our revelation.

After we filled them in on what we found, I asked, "Did you see anything on the camera footage?"

"Not really," Seamus said. "I'll show yeh."

The great part about the camera systems on the estate was they were all connected and easily accessed on

Gráinne, Donal, and Seamus's phones, in addition to being accessible from the television screen in the sitting room. I didn't have my own personal log in, and I felt weird asking for it. Especially since we weren't yet married.

He went to the twenty-four hours before Wes was arrested. We watched as people drove by. Wes left and went to the barns, then came back. Not one of the cars that drove up stopped at his house. And Gráinne, Donal, or Seamus easily identified every car.

I sucked in a breath and let it out with a big sigh. "Well, that was anti-climactic."

"Maybe they snuck in the back?" Rylie suggested.

"It's possible," Gráinne said. "But we checked the other camera angles, and it seems pretty quiet."

"Did the cameras come back right when the power came back on?" I asked.

Seamus went back to where there was a gap in the timeline. When he pressed play on the one that showed Wes's house most directly, it was in line with when the power turned back on.

"Can we watch from this point on?" I asked. "We can go fast, but I want to see what happens with Wes. At this time, he was at Harry's, right?"

"From what we know, yes," Seamus said. "He went to Harry's after discovering what happened to Sophie."

"And proceeded to tell the entire world how he was responsible for her death," Gráinne said, frustration and desperation in her tone.

"What's that?" I asked as a car pulled up around two in the morning.

"Looks like whoever brought Wes home that night," Donal said. "I'm glad he wasn't out driving himself."

The driver's side door opened, and someone I least expected to see stepped out.

A man in a cowboy hat.

25

"Vince brought Wes home that night?" Gráinne asked.

It almost looked like Vince was carrying Wes.

"He looks passed out," Rylie said.

Vince was only inside for a few minutes before he returned to his car.

"Okay, that's suspicious," I said. "Did Wes know Vince was trying to buy Boo-Boo?"

"I'd mentioned it, but if he didn't give Wes his real name, Wes might not have known," Gráinne said.

"Or cared," Donal said. "I know if something happened to yeh, Love, I'd be distraught. It wouldn't matter who had to scrape me off the concrete. I probably wouldn't have the mind to care."

"'Tis true," Seamus said, reaching down and squeezing my hand.

Rylie averted her eyes.

"What is he doing?" I asked as Vince got back out of the car.

"He has something in his arms," Rylie said. "A box."

She wiggled her eyebrows at me. We were thinking the same thing. That was likely the box of horseshoes and drugs. Vince had planted them there.

"It looks like he's wearing gloves, too," Seamus pointed out. "That's suspicious, right?"

Twenty minutes of footage later, Vince walked back out, got in his truck, and left.

"If that's not proof of wrongdoing, I don't know what is," Donal said. "We need to get this footage over to Molly right away."

"What was he carrying in the box?" Gráinne asked, giving Rylie and me the stink eye. Her mom radar was going off. She knew we were withholding something.

"We can't tell you," I said. "I'm really sorry."

"Does it have something to do with the blood test yeh didn't want me to have done on Boo-Boo?"

"I forgot to ask—did you have it done?" I asked.

"I did," she said. "And Boo-Boo came back clear other than a mild sedative, which I suspect Wes gave him after the incident to keep him calm."

I pulled the folder of papers from my purse and looked through them. "Did they test for psuedolisitine?"

Gráinne's eyebrows came together in the middle of her forehead. "Of course not. I'd never give my horses psuedolisitine. It's illegal for one. And what is it yer looking at?"

"Psuedolisitine doesn't show up on some regular tests," I said gently.

"How do yeh—what are yeh—he wouldn't have had it in his blood." Gráinne was flustered.

I glanced at Rylie.

"The two of yeh better come clean right now," Gráinne said in the same tone she'd used when she'd kicked Vince out of the box on New Year's Day after he'd cursed in her presence.

"I can't tell you everything," I said. "I made a promise, and I'd like to keep it. But I do know that Tilda's been drugging her horses, and there's a chance those same drugs somehow ended up in Boo-Boo's bloodstream."

Gráinne sat down as if she might pass out. "That can't be. Is that why she's been winning so much?"

"It's probably one factor," I said. "The other being that she's not racing against the best horses in the business."

Gráinne gave me a small smile. "But are they the best because Wes had been drugging them? Is that what they found in his house?"

"I don't think Wes had been drugging the horses," I said. "Even if that is what they found in his house. Not saying it is, but even if that is."

I was toeing a fine line between keeping a secret and not.

"Vince is setting him up," Seamus said. "I bet he called Sophie from the bar to distract her when she was in the barn."

"Tilda's in on it, too," I said. "Rylie and I watched the race footage from the day Sophie was murdered, and Tilda wasn't in the winner's circle."

"She wasn't?" Donal asked. "But everyone said they saw her there."

"She could have been there at the start or the end of the race," I said. "It was only up in Northern Ireland."

"And about the sedative," Rylie said. "I don't think Wes gave Boo-Boo anything that night. He was already drunk when he got to the barn."

"It would make sense for someone to give Boo-Boo the drug so they could kill Sophie without him trampling them," I said. "Remember when we went in the barn, and all the other horses were freaking out, but Boo-Boo was practically a statue?"

"Let's get all this down to Molly," Seamus said. "Tonight. We have to go to the garda station tonight."

We walked up to the front desk of the station, where a bored-looking officer sat clicking around on a computer.

"Excuse me," I said. "We're here about the Sophie Walsh case. We have some new evidence to present."

The officer peered up at us over his glasses. "Who's the investigating officer?"

"Molly Ryan," I replied.

He nodded and picked up the phone, dialing an extension. "Molly, some people here say they have new evidence on your case . . . okay."

Hanging up, he turned back to us. "She's tied up at the moment. You can have a seat, and she'll be out when she can."

I glanced anxiously at Rylie. We needed to talk to someone now.

After a few minutes of tense waiting, I couldn't take it anymore. I marched back up to the desk.

"Sorry, officer, but we need to speak with someone immediately," I insisted. "This is time-sensitive information."

He gave me an indifferent look. "Like I said, you'll have to wait for Molly."

Frustration boiled up inside me. I placed my hands firmly on the desk and lowered my voice. "Listen, a dangerous killer is still out there. Are you really going to shrug off potential evidence that could get them off the streets?"

The officer straightened up, finally looking me in the eye. "No need for theatrics, ma'am. I'll see who else is available."

"Thank you," I replied.

He picked up the phone again, speaking in a hushed tone. After a moment, he hung up.

"Detective Green can speak with you briefly. Second door on the left."

We followed his directions to a small office. The detective, a bald man with a mustache, sat scribbling notes. He glanced up impatiently as we entered.

"What can I do for you?"

I quickly launched into an explanation about the evidence we'd found.

He listened with a stone-faced expression, the scratches of his pen on paper grating on my nerves. I wished I could snatch the notepad away to see what he was writing.

When I finished, he didn't speak for several uncomfortable moments. Just as I was about to prompt him again, he finally said in a bored tone, "This all sounds very speculative. Now, if you have any concrete evidence . . ."

My anxiety snapped, giving way to anger. "Speculative?" I argued. "This directly links Tilda to the crime scene at the time of the murder. You need to bring her in for questioning."

"I'll pass your . . . theories along to Molly," he said dismissively.

"Theories?" I threw my hands up. "This is cold, hard evidence. Tilda did this, and you're just sitting here, not caring a killer is walking free!"

Rylie put a gentle hand on my shoulder. "Shayla, let's go. He said he'll tell Molly."

I bit my tongue, glaring at the indifferent detective. We'd done everything short of dragging the suspect in, yet still justice eluded us. Turning sharply, we walked out.

I fumed the entire way back to the car. The Gardaí's inaction might allow the killer to slip away forever. We couldn't let that happen - we had to find another way.

I thought Molly would call first thing in the morning. Or at least one of the other officers. But we heard nothing. Gráinne decided to get all the horses explicitly tested for psuedolisitine, just in case. It was a risk, but she didn't want to race a horse that wasn't legally fit to run.

"Tilda should be back in town by now, right?" Rylie asked as we walked through what was left of the castle. It had burned down recently and would have to be renovated. "Maybe we should pay her a visit."

"The only problem is, I don't know where to start."

"Does she have a business location? Or maybe Gráinne knows where she lives?"

"If I ask Gráinne where she lives or works, Gráinne will freak out and tell us not to confront her."

"I mean, maybe it's not the safest thing, but if we're together, it would be better than going alone," Rylie said with a shrug.

"It would be even better if the Gardaí took us seriously."

I'd called the station, called Molly, and texted Molly multiple times but got absolutely nothing.

After a moment, I pulled out my phone and tapped on the Instagram app.

"Ooh, good idea. Maybe she posted something," Rylie said.

The most recent picture on Tilda's vibrant Instagram feed was a photo of her and several other women. The caption read: *Watch us play at Ballywick Greenway today at two.*

"Bingo. She's playing some sort of sport at the greenway today."

I showed Rylie the photo.

"That's cricket," Rylie said. "The bats are flat and wooden. Kind of like paddles."

I looked at the picture again. "What if she nailed a horseshoe to the bat and used it to hit Sophie?"

"That makes sense. And it's clever because just that action would spook Boo-Boo enough to step on her a couple of times. I bet that's where the horseshoe nail came from, too."

"She must have hit Sophie pretty hard," I said, wincing at the thought.

"Maybe she died quicker that way," Rylie said, trying to find the sun through the rain. "Let's get over there."

26

The game had already begun when we arrived at the greenway. The sun cast a weak glow over the park. Even in this season, the grass remained stubbornly green. The only people out were the two teams and a handful of spectators with their jackets drawn around them to protect them from the slight chill in the air.

Tilda was on the field playing a strange-looking version of baseball with the paddle-like cricket bats. She easily held the polished bat, her muscles flexing as she prepared to swing.

"Do you think her truck is unlocked?" Rylie asked. "We could do a little digging while she's playing."

"Maybe, but how will we know which one is her truck?" I glanced through the parking lot, then realized what I'd missed. A bright red truck with the words Tilda Williams and what I assumed was her business phone number were spelled out in big white letters and numbers. "Ah, right. That one."

Rylie and I tried to act as casually as possible as we made our way over. If only I could have quieted my thudding heart. What if she noticed us? But the thrill of possibly finding clues overrode my caution.

"Let's just look in the windows and see what we can find," I said. "We don't want to disturb evidence."

Rylie nodded in agreement. Though, I wasn't confident she'd actually stay out of the truck if nothing was visible from the windows. Her eyes held a determined glint. Subtlety wasn't her strong suit when justice was on the line.

The truck was so tall neither of us could easily see inside without stepping up on the side rails. I jumped up and flung myself into the truck's bed while she tried to peek in the overly tinted passenger side window while holding onto the mirror and the door handle so she wouldn't fall backward.

I stayed as low as possible so no one would see me in the back. The truck bed contained only a few tools and a spare tire. Nothing incriminating.

"Do you see anything?" I whispered.

"No," Rylie whispered back. "The windows are too dark."

"Same here. I need a flashlight or something."

Rylie didn't reply. It wasn't like she would just have a flashlight on her person. She wasn't in her ranger uniform.

I crawled over to the other side. Maybe something was physically blocking the back window in this spot. Still no luck.

"I can't see anything," Rylie said. "Do you think we should open the doors?"

"I wouldn't do that if I were you," a high-pitched voice said behind me. I flattened myself in the truck's bed as I heard the door pop open and what sounded like Rylie landing on her butt.

"What are you doing peeking in my truck windows?" The voice was the same one from the day of the New Year's Race—Tilda. She slammed the door shut so hard it rattled the entire truck. "I'll ask one more time. What are you doing looking in the windows of my truck?"

Tilda was past the bed now. I had to do something before she used the flat bat in her hands on Rylie. Fury boiled inside me. She wouldn't hurt my friend.

I peeked over the side to find Rylie still on her butt, with junk scattered around her.

Tilda hovered above Rylie with her flat bat held high. Her eyes blazed with contempt, oblivious to anything around her.

"I-I wasn't doing anything," Rylie said, crab-walking backward.

It was now or never.

I launched myself out of the truck bed and tackled Tilda. We tumbled to the pavement as I wrenched the bat from her grasp.

Rylie scrambled to her feet to help me keep Tilda on the ground.

"What are you doing?" Tilda shouted. "Help! They're attacking me."

When the garda car drove up behind her truck, she started wiggling.

"Stop moving." Rylie pinned Tilda's flailing legs while I kept her arms subdued.

"Help! Gardaí! I'm right here."

Molly got out and walked slowly over to us.

"Thank God you got here in time," Tilda said. "These two were peeking in my truck windows, and then they attacked me."

"Oh right, like you weren't going to hit me with your bat," Rylie said. "Just like you hit Sophie. Only this bat doesn't have a horseshoe nailed to it."

Tilda stopped wiggling. "I don't know what you're talking about."

"Yes, you do," I said. "You weren't at that race. You weren't on the winner's circle footage. You were in the O'Malley stables, drugging Boo-Boo and attacking Sophie."

Her lies only fueled my determination to expose the truth.

"That's ridiculous," Tilda said. "Made up stories."

"And then Vince just happened to take Wes home from the bar that night, giving him the perfect opportunity to plant evidence in Wes's house," Rylie continued.

"You're not going to believe them, are you?" Tilda asked Molly.

I looked up at the woman who had been avoiding me for the past twenty-four hours.

"Tilda Williams, yer under arrest for murder," Molly finally said.

Molly cuffed Tilda before we let her up.

"You have to be kidding me," Tilda said. "I was out of the country when she died. People saw me at that race."

"Out of the country, as in Northern Ireland," I said.

"And I'd venture to guess the flight logs on your private jet will tell a different story." Rylie smiled. "Unless you destroyed them. But there's always asking the pilot. Unless you killed him, too."

Molly shook her head. "That's enough. We have plenty of evidence, including a flight log and evidence of a money transfer to someone who works in the same electric company that powers the O'Malley estate. If we go through everything in yer truck and yer home, I'm guessing we'll find the murder weapon."

I kicked at a bat that fell out of the backseat and flipped it over with my toe. A horseshoe complete with silver nails—one missing—and an engraved star was nailed to the flat side of the bat.

"I can explain that," Tilda said.

"Let's go," Molly said, leading Tilda to the garda car.

"Good work," Rylie said. "I'm impressed."

"We make a good team," I said.

"Yeh certainly do," Molly said, coming back over. "But what were yeh thinking confronting Tilda like that?"

"If you would have replied, we wouldn't have," I said. "We couldn't let her roam free to kill someone else."

"What were yeh gonna do with her?" Molly said. "Tie her up in the back of yer car?"

I glanced at Rylie, who shrugged. Apparently, neither of us had gotten that far.

"I'll be more careful next time," I said.

"Let's hope there isn't a next time," Molly said.

"Right, you know what I—yeah."

Molly smiled. "I'm just coddin' yeh."

"You should also check the medication she's been giving her horses," I said. "And lock up Vince, too. We have video proof that he planted the box of horseshoes in Wes's house."

Molly nodded. "Will do."

Rylie and I stood, smiling as she got in the police car and took Tilda away.

27

When I walked through the front door, Gráinne wrapped me in a massive hug. "Yeh did it. I'm so proud."

She let me go and moved on to hug Rylie. "And you too!"

"No, no," Rylie said. "It was all Shayla. I might have met the same fate as Sophie if she hadn't been there. You should have seen her tackle Tilda. It was epic."

"You wouldn't have died," I said. "She would have taken one swing, and you would have taken her down."

Rylie shrugged. "I guess we'll never know. You probably just saved my life. I owe you one."

"How about you pay me back by being my maid of honor?"

Rylie's eyes filled with tears as she nearly tackled me in a big bear hug.

"I'll take that as a yes?"

"Yes!" Rylie shouted. "Yes! Yes!"

We jumped around excitedly.

"Now, will you show me your cottage?" Rylie asked when we finished celebrating.

"That'll have to come a bit later," Gráinne said. "Right now, I want yeh to come with me."

"Where's Seamus?" I asked.

"He and Donal went to retrieve Wes from the police station," she said. "We'll give him a grand welcome home reception tonight, but it could take a bit to release him."

She motioned for Rylie and me to follow her upstairs. I'd never been in Gráinne and Donal's room before.

Stepping into the primary suite, I was immediately taken aback by its sheer opulence. Every detail screamed luxury, from the shimmering gold trims to the plush king-sized bed draped in the softest silks. You'd never guess from how humble Gráinne and Donal were that this was where they slept every night.

"Come on, it's in here," Gráinne said, pushing through the closet door to reveal a gigantic walk-in closet. Rows of designer outfits, shoes, and accessories were meticulously displayed as if we were in a museum. But the door opened at the back of the closet was what caught my eye most.

My heart raced as I followed Gráinne through what was probably a concealed door when closed. Before me lay a room filled with jewelry that could rival any high-end boutique. The sparkle of diamonds, the glow of gold, the allure of pearls; it was overwhelming in the best possible way.

"This is my private collection," Gráinne said. "I don't wear a lot of jewelry, but I like to go all out when I do."

A warm feeling surged within me, not just because of the treasures before me but the thought of the stories they held—the memories they represented. Among the glitz and glamour, there was a heart.

"I want yeh to choose what to wear for your wedding," Gráinne said. "Nothing is off limits, and whatever yeh choose will be yers to keep."

My jaw hung open. How was this even happening? Was I going to wake up from a dream where we hadn't caught Tilda, and I wasn't about to pick out the most expensive piece of . . . anything . . . I'd ever owned?

"I don't even know where to start," I said, glancing at Rylie.

"Don't look at me," Rylie said. "I'm about as knowledgeable about jewelry as I am about exotic lizards."

"How are yeh going to wear yer hair?" Gráinne asked.

"I thought I'd put it in a low bun like I had it when we went shopping, but I've been thinking of keeping it down. What do you think?"

Rylie and Gráinne exchanged a look, and both said, "Down," in unison.

"Down it is," I said with a laugh.

"If yeh wear it down, I think a tiara might be a pleasant touch." Gráinne motioned to a case with five headpieces ranging from tiny to full crowns.

"Wow," I said. "Are you sure? I'm happy just to borrow something and give it back."

"In my family, this is how we do things. I don't want my children to have to wait until I'm dead to inherit my belongings. I'd much rather see them used and loved while I'm alive."

I glanced at Rylie. "What do you think?"

Rylie examined the headpieces. "With your hair, I

think you need something a bit bigger. Not as big as the crown, but maybe one of those two?" She pointed to two of the tiaras in the middle.

One was loops of diamonds with tiny pearls in the center of each loop. The other was more colorful, with a mixture of diamonds and emeralds.

"I love that one," I said, pointing at the one with the emeralds. "It reminds me of Ireland."

When I looked up at Gráinne, she had a tear in her eye and a wide smile. "That's the one I thought you might choose. It belonged to Maeve—my great-grandmother. No one has worn it since her wedding ages ago."

"It's so perfect," I said. "I can't believe no one has worn it."

"There's a story behind why it's not been worn," Gráinne said. "It was lost for many years. Actually, all of Maeve's possessions were. It was thought the items had been lost for good, but a few years ago, we received this anonymous package with her jewelry, journals, and other things perfectly preserved. We still don't know how they got here or who brought them. One of the things in the package was a picture of Maeve wearing that crown on her wedding day."

"I'd be honored to wear it," I said. "Thank you so much. I'll take the best care of it."

"I have no doubts," Gráinne said. "But that's not all. Yeh need to choose earrings, a necklace, and a bracelet if you'd like."

"You're better at this than I am," I said to Gráinne. "And there are just so many beautiful, sparkly things. Can you give me some options that you think would go well with my dress and the tiara?"

Gráinne rubbed her hands together. "Let's see." She looked around the display cases, considering every item as if she'd never seen them before. "For the earrings, since yer hair will be down, yeh'll probably want something small. Maybe even studs. Yeh could go with simple diamond solitaires." She pointed at a pair of massive diamond earrings. "Or something that hangs down a bit that ties in the emeralds in the tiara."

The emerald earrings were teardrop-shaped, with diamonds surrounding the emerald stone.

"Ooh, wait, I have a set. I almost forgot about it." She rushed to one of the back cases. "I'm not telling yeh what to do, but look at these."

She pulled out a box that contained a long necklace with tiny diamonds all the way around and earrings that had the same tiny diamonds that would hang down about two inches from my ears.

"They're perfect," I said.

Gráinne closed the box and handed it to me. "They're yours."

"Where did these come from?" I asked.

"They were a gift from my father when I started the business," she said. "Yeh would have loved him."

I threw my arms around Gráinne's neck. She laughed and hugged me back.

Wes, Donal, and Seamus sat at the large dining room table when we returned downstairs. Magella walked in, holding a large silver tray with a domed lid as if she could sense we'd arrived.

"We're so happy to have yeh back, Wes," Gráinne said, patting him on the shoulder before taking her seat at the head of the table. "I'm so sorry about Sophie."

Magella lifted the lid to show a roasted turkey surrounded by roasted veggies.

"My favorite," Wes said. "Thank yeh, Magella."

Magella beamed at him. "I couldn't let yeh return from jail without a hearty meal prepared."

"I can't believe you're leaving tomorrow," I said to Rylie as everyone else was busy filling their plates with the aromatic food.

"I'll be back before you know it," she said. "I have a bachelorette party to plan, a bridal shower to attend, and, of course, the wedding."

"Well, schedule some extra time because there's a lot to see in Ireland that we didn't get to see this time."

She slipped an arm around my shoulders. "Just seeing you was enough for me."

As we gobbled down our food, Donal said, "I hope losing Sophie was all the bad luck we have coming for us this year."

Rylie and I exchanged a glance. We quickly rapped our knuckles on the table.

"Knock on wood," we said together.

ACKNOWLEDGMENTS

Thank you to my amazing family. I love that I get to write every day and call it a job.

Massive thanks to my sister for getting me all the horse information I needed for this book.

Thank you to my readers, friends, and fellow authors—especially the ones who cheer me on day in and day out.

Thank you, God. For literally everything.

ABOUT THE AUTHOR

Stella Bixby is a native Coloradan who loves to snowboard, pluck at the guitar, and play board games with her family. She was once a volunteer firefighter and a park ranger, but now spends most of her time making up stories and trying to figure out what to cook for dinner.

Connect with Stella on Facebook, Twitter, and Instagram @StellaBixby.

Stella loves to hear from her readers!
www.stellabixby.com

ALSO BY STELLA BIXBY

Rylie Cooper Series

Catfished: Book 1

Suckered: Book 2

Throttled: Book 3

Tampered: Book 4

Whacked: Book 5

Bungled: Book 6

Snowed: Book 7

Wasted: Book 8

Booked: Book 9

Signed: Book 10

Haunted: Book 11

Shayla Murphy Series

Mistletoe Malarkey: Book 1

Hooved Homicide: Book 2

Veiled Vengeance: Book 3

Muddy Murder: Book 4

Celtic Clue: Book 5

Magical Mane Mystery Series

Downward Death: Book 1

Bowling Blunder: Book 2

Spotlight Scandal: Book 3

Tango Trouble: Book 4

Spelunking Speculations: Book 5

Festival Fiasco: Book 6

Jamboree Justice: Book 7

Cosmic Conspiracy: Book 8

Bonfire Betrayal: Book 9

Printed in Great Britain
by Amazon